ERADICATING DARKNESS

A DONATELLA GRIPPING THRILLER

DEMETRIUS JACKSON

PROLOGUE

Detective Carl Sampson could feel the blood pressing against his eardrums as he mopped the mixture of rain, sweat, and concrete dust from his brows. He watched helplessly as Nurse Jasmyn did her best to revive her good friend and his new...

Where the hell is that ambulance? he thought, anxiously awaiting its arrival. He could hear the sirens whirring in the distance, but they didn't appear to be getting any closer.

"Come on, Donatella," he said, pounding the ground soaked in rain and mud. "You can't let this son of a bitch win!"

With the flurry of activity they endured, he hadn't taken inventory of himself or his injuries and soon realized with the impact that he'd dislocated his shoulder. The adrenaline coursing through his body had negated the pain, but the dull ache was preparing to emerge as excruciating pain.

The reflection of the lights emanating from the ambulance cleared his thoughts. "They're here," he exclaimed, pushing himself to his feet and blocking away the pain. He waved them down as they approached and slowed to a stop.

Out of habit, he reached for his shield before recalling he didn't have it. "Detective Sampson," he said behind clenched teeth. "Hurry, she's right here." He pointed the emergency crew in the direction of Jasmyn, who was hunched over the prone motionless form of Donatella.

With practiced motion, the pair opened the rear doors and retrieved the gurney.

Jasmyn stood and spoke, "Black female, age twenty-nine, excellent physical health. Injected with unknown substance, currently unresponsive but still breathing."

The techs maneuvered her into position and quickly strapped her into place. They lifted it back to full height and began rolling it to the ambulance.

"Thanks, we've got it from here," one of the techs said as they slid the gurney into the back.

"I'm coming with you," Jasmyn said as they prepared to climb in. "I'm a nurse at Atrium and the victim's friend. I can lend a hand."

The techs shot each other a glance and wordlessly agreed to the request.

"So am I," Sampson said as Jasmyn climbed in.

"Wait a minute," the tech said. "we don't have the room and aren't allowed to have civilians riding with us."

"Make the room," he said in a cold, menacing tone.

The tech parted her lips to say something but thought better of it and simply slid to the side to let him enter.

By the time he was in and the door was closed, Donatella's shirt had been cut open, and EKG leads had been placed across her chest. Her pulse was thready, and her blood pressure was spiking.

In the bright lights, he could see how much color had drained from her face. *Come on, fight*, he thought as he watched them work.

The activity picked up suddenly, and distantly he heard Jasmyn shout, "We're losing her!"

His eyes grew wide, and a ping of pain registered in his chest. *Not again, not another one.* His mind flashed back to when Porter was in an ambulance fighting for her life and how helpless he'd been to save her.

He watched as Jasmyn fought to insert an IV into her vein. His focus shifted to the ever-slowing heart rate monitor and the rhythm that decreased with each subsequent beat of her heart.

His eyes turned back to Jasmyn and the techs as their urgency reached a fevered pitch. Guilt began to creep into his mind for placing her in the path of this psychopath. If only...

The slow, rhythmic report from the heart monitor beeped once more before giving way to the monotoned flatline.

1

Special Agent Donatella Dabria placed a fresh log on the embers smoldering within the fireplace. She rearranged the logs using the bronze poker forged of high-density tungsten metal from her fireplace set. Satisfied that the blaze would once again renew, she returned to her midnight-black Malibu Chesterfield Chair, crossed her left leg over her right, and spoke in her honeyed southern drawl.

"Please, start from the beginning."

She eyed the man sitting across from her as he mentally wrestled with the words to convey the thoughts racing through his mind. He parted his lips to speak, but before he could come out with anything, he ever so slowly closed them again. His eyes shifted from a distant spot over her right shoulder to the fire building in the fireplace, purposefully avoiding eye contact with her.

This visit was an unexpected one. Months had passed since the special agent and the detective had last seen one another and even longer since the ordeal they had with

Terri Buckley at the Cleveland Museum of Art, one in which she nearly met her end. The determination and confidence he'd shown in bringing that episode to an end was unrecognizable in the detective present today.

The silence grew with each passing moment as the seconds felt like minutes, the minutes like hours. Sampson shifted in his chair, dropped his head and in a barely audible voice, and said, "It never should have gotten to this."

His shoulders rose as he inhaled deeply and then dropped as he slowly pushed the air back out.

"The first murder scene was as gruesome as it was shocking. The victim, a college coed, had been missing without a trace. And then out of the blue her mutilated body had been found." He snorted. "'Found' wouldn't exactly be correct. The killer displayed her body in a public setting for all the world to see."

He shifted again, head still lowered. "As we continued to investigate, the clues began to point us toward a likely suspect, but I couldn't shake the feeling that something wasn't right. My boss was convinced in the suspect's guilt and demanded that we proceed and wrap it up quickly."

Sampson lifted his head and his eyes, red and focused, connecting with hers. She could feel both the pain and hatred behind his glare.

"So, we did. We focused our investigation on the suspect that was being dangled out in front of us, gathered all the evidence that pointed toward his guilt, and ultimately made our arrest. My chief was happy, the mayor was happy, and we received attaboys from the department and the public," he said, brows furrowed and eyes narrowing. "But the night of the arrest, I received a call from a private number. The caller, the killer, confirmed my suspicions that the person we arrested was innocent. At least innocent of the crime he was in jail for. He also mentioned he'd already abducted his next victim and said that if I could not find her in time, she would face the same end."

As he talked, Donatella was careful not to interrupt but mentally categorized the facts for later use.

"After the rush to judgment from my superior, I took it upon myself to investigate this latest abduction. I was determined to find her. I would not allow her to be killed and skinned by that sick bastard," he said, lowering his voice again. "But I failed."

He closed his eyes, and the room dropped into an eerie quiet. The ringing of Sampson's mobile phone brought the silence to an end. He retrieved the phone from his pocket. "Sampson," he said upon answering. He listened as the caller spoke and then simply said, "I'll be there shortly."

He reopened his eyes, connecting them with Donatella's. "I'm wanted at HQ." He rose from his seat as she did the same. "We must put an end to this monster, whatever it takes. I will not see him hurt anyone else."

"We will," she agreed as she walked him to the door. "I have a colleague in the FBI who may be able to help us in this matter. Let's reconvene once you're finished at headquarters."

He nodded in agreement, opened the door, and proceeded to his car. She closed the door behind him and began to replay the conversation in her head. She couldn't shake the feeling that he wasn't telling her the whole story. Furthermore, on several occasions he said "we" in referring to the case, but to her knowledge Sampson didn't work with a partner. At least none that she was aware of.

A STALE BREEZE filled the room from the forced air being blown through the ceiling vents. The unidentified assailant sits in his oversized chair, feet propped on the brown leather ottoman. He presses rewind on the Roku remote, replaying the news coverage from the previous day. Sure, there has been additional coverage regarding the death of the officer, but nothing compares to the frantic scene that unfolded in real-time.

"Sherry Long on scene at 2821 Turtle Drive of what can only be described as a horrific turn of events. Detective Elise Porter, a first-year detective with Charlotte Metro Police Department, has been whisked away in an ambulance. She'd been abducted from her hotel room while she waited to close on this residential property. The department's search for her whereabouts brought them to this home where she was found, bound and unresponsive. We arrived to an array of red and blue lights illuminating the night sky in time to witness the ambulance pulling away. Her status is unknown, but suffice it to say, from the tone of everyone around, her survival is in question.

We haven't been about to garner an official response, but from what we've been able to gather, her partner, Detective Carl Sampson, forced his way into the back of the ambulance to be with her. We – Wait a minute, there appears to be commotion going on behind us."

The camera swings in the direction Captain Marshall and the disorder around him. Sherry and her cameraman hurry in that direction.

"Captain, has there been any update on Detective Porter's condition?"

All action simultaneously stopped as the image focused in on the captain. His trademark stern demeanor took on a different look, a more solemn look.

"We received word that Detective Porter didn't make it to the hospital. CMPD has lost a sister in arms and a wonderful human being."

The unsub played back the last segment once again, listening to the captain's lament with relish.

He paused the video at the perfect spot to capture the anguish, despair, and realization that the captain had failed one of his subordinates. The only thing that would have been better was to capture the look on Sampson's face when his partner took her last breath.

He wanted to revel in the satisfaction of this hunt and its outcome, but the voice was already back in his head. *She was indeed a worthy adversary, but we can do better. It's time we start hunting for our next prey. A bigger, more formidable challenge.*

Typically, a quarrel would ignite as the voice in his head spoke, but not on this occasion. In fact, he had been pondering the same thing. Who could fit the criteria? Who would be a bigger conquest than a detective whose sole job was to find him?

"I'll need to contemplate this for a while," he said out loud as he picked up the Roku remote and pressed the red power button extinguishing the light from the television and plunging the room into darkness.

2

Veronica King sat in her redesigned office at Global Insight Security, tapping the desk with the gold custom pen she received for her fifth anniversary with the company. There hadn't been any blowback from the death of Lydia Brooks, and to her knowledge it was still being considered a tragic accident.

She'd forgotten how potent a set of carefully curated chemicals could be when mixed with the proper concentrations. Ridding herself of Lydia was only the first step. Now as she sat in her office, she contemplated her next move.

Susan, the head of The Syndicate, would not go down so easily. It would take a much more elaborate plan to both remove her from service and get in position to replace her. Veronica had a taste of that power and now wanted more.

Last night, she studied the available white papers and dark websites on chemicals and compounds she was unfamiliar with. A lot had changed since her college days, and it was important for her that she was educated on the latest compounds, their properties, and most importantly their warnings. She jotted and organized copious notes in the One Note application on her computer. Its autosave feature ensured she wouldn't lose anything because she'd forgotten to periodically save the file. Her thought process was interrupted when her executive assistant, Derrick West, knocked on the partially ajar door.

"Yes," she said distractedly, managing a glance in his direction.

"Ms. King," he said in his husky voice, "Han Zhiwang and the remainder of the Chinese contingent will arrive within the hour. I've set them up in the executive conference room, and the breakfast you have requested will arrive in the next five minutes. I believe everything is set for your meeting. Would you like me to sit in with you as well?"

"That won't be necessary. Today, we will finalize the contract to overhaul their security. This should be a straightforward conversation."

"If you need anything I'll be close by. All you need to do is ring me, and I'll be right there."

"Thank you, Derrick," she said as she watched him walk back to his desk. She had to admit she understood why her female employees visited during the workday. His broad shoulders, athletic build, and dimpled ass made him hard to resist. And with all the physical qualities, he knew how to handle a gun and was a master at jiujitsu. She made the mental note to incorporate him into her plan to take down Susan.

For now, she needed to focus on closing the deal with Zhiwang, then she'd have plenty of time to devise her next steps to become the leader of The Syndicate.

THE SMELL of freshly brewed coffee and homemade pastries permeated through Brent's Coffee Shop, captivating those who waited in line to place their orders.

"It always smells so good in here," the woman in front of Jasmyn Thompson stated to her friend next to her.

"I'm convinced they have a hidden blower tucked away within the walls to push that smell out to us," the friend commented, taking another step forward, now next in line.

"I swear the main reason I work out as hard as I do is so I can have one of those cinnamon rolls twice a week and not feel guilty. It takes my supreme willpower not to order that and a cranberry walnut muffin."

"Next in line," the barista called in the direction of the chatty friends.

Jasmyn, who was next up, was now left with a conundrum. The talk of the cinnamon rolls and muffins left her teetering on a decision. She had every intention of only coming in for a tea, but now as the moment of truth was arriving, she could sense her willpower slipping away.

"Next in line," the barista called once again, and mounting pressure of a decision had come at last. She didn't want to be one of those people who stood in line all this time and still didn't know what she wanted when it was her turn. Nonetheless, she stared at the menu as if it just appeared once she reached the counter. She measured her steps while simultaneously turning the decision over and over in her head.

When she reached the counter she said, "A medium green iced tea, please."

"Coming right up," the barista said, keying in her order before walking away to make the drink. In that moment, Jasmyn was proud of herself. She didn't succumb to the pressure and would walk away with what she planned to purchase. She watched as the women in front of her received a heated cinnamon roll, the icing dripping down to the plate.

"Would you like anything else?" the barista asked, sliding her drink across the counter.

"Yeah, I'll take a cinnamon roll for here."

"Would you like it heated?"

"Absolutely!"

"Coming right up."

I'll hold out next time, she thought as she unlocked her cell phone so her app could be scanned.

With drink and food in hand, Jasmyn was now in search of a place to sit. She was headed to an open table in the corner when she heard someone call, "Jasmyn, is that you?"

She turned in the direction of the voice to find Bethany Evans sitting at a table by the window.

"Oh my God, girl, it is you." Bethany stood and pulled Jasmyn into a warm embrace. "If you're looking for a spot to sit, I'm here all alone this morning."

Jasmyn set her drink and roll on the table, slung her crossbody over the back of the chair, and plopped down in the seat. "It's so good to see you, Beth. It's been way too long."

"Yes, it has. I saw that husband of yours strapping your son into the car seat a few weeks back. He's getting so big!"

Jasmyn couldn't help but to smile. "Yes, he is. It's hard to believe he's already walking and talking. I can see his little mind working to solve life's mysteries." The two shared a laugh, and Jasmyn asked, "How's your little one?"

"She's good. I left her with the nanny this morning so I can get away from the house for a while. My feet have been dying for a pedicure, so I booked the first appointment of the morning. Then I decided to treat myself to one of Brent's delectable treats." She glanced down at Jasmyn's cinnamon roll nearly activating her Pavlovian response.

"After this, I'm picking up Troy's dry cleaning and then heading back home."

Jasmyn finished the bite she'd taken and asked, "How's Troy doing these days?"

"Great! He's teaching over at UNCC, and Emily is the apple of her father's eye. I know it's only a matter of time until she supplants me as his favorite girl, but until that day comes, he's all mine." The two shared a heartfelt laugh and carried on the conversation for another thirty minutes.

"Look at the time," Beth said while gathering her belongings. "I told the nanny I'd only be gone ninety minutes max ,and it's been almost three hours." Jasmyn piled her cup onto the empty plate and unslung her purse from the chair.

They both stood, and Beth said, "Let's be sure to catch up more frequently. I miss having adult conversations throughout the day."

"How about we meet here again next week around the same time?" Jasmyn suggested.

Bethany considered it for a moment and then said, "Why the hell not?"

They both embraced in a hug, and then Bethany headed for the exit while Jasmyn took her plate and cup to the dish-collecting counter. As she did, she was already planning a get together in her head with friends and family.

3

The early morning air was crisp with a hint of moisture building when Donatella set out for her 5:00 a.m. run. But now, at a quarter to nine, as she stood outside of her Audi R8 Spyder awaiting the arrival of Detective Sampson, the temperature had increased by twenty degrees. The high for the day threatened to top out around 96, and humidity was high as well. She'd lived in the south her entire life and was accustomed to the heat, but when the air was stale and the wind circulating the city was at a minimum, the heat and humidity seemed to entomb you in a virtual inferno. It hadn't reached that point yet, but by noon she was sure that would be the case.

Sampson pulled into the parking spot next to hers and stepped out of the car with coffee in hand. "Good morning," he said in a semi-strained voice that didn't escape Donatella's ears. She gave him a quick once-over, sensing something was off but not wanting to pry.

She said, "Last night after your departure, I contacted a colleague, Agent H.E. Browning. She's the best criminal profiler in the country, and I've had the pleasure of working with her to solve numerous cases. I gave her a rundown, advised her that time was of the essence, and informed her we would stop by at 9:00 to obtain her thoughts."

"Do you think that's enough time?" Sampson asked before taking a sip from his cup.

"There's no doubt in my mind she'll have something tangible for us to proceed with. As we continue to feed her information, she'll be able to get us more actionable intelligence."

Sampson drained the remainder of his drink, tossed the cup into the nearby recycling bin, and said, "Well, let's see what she has to offer. After you."

Donatella led Sampson into the new FBI building, where they stopped at the front desk. Detective Sampson signed in. After the destruction of their previous location, security had been considerably tightened up. All visitors needed to be retrieved from the lobby, and the agent responsible for the visitor had to swipe their badge and complete a retinal scan. Donatella completed both, and Sampson was issued a visitors' badge.

Browning was located on the southwest wing of the second floor, so Donatella and Sampson proceeded to the open staircase to climb the steps. At the top, they rescanned their badges. This granted them access to the corridor for Browning's office. Sampson noticed agents focused on their work behind the glass enclosures and that each room required another scan of the badge. About three-quarters of the way down the corridor, they arrived at a door marked "Behavioral Analysis." They scanned their badges once again and entered.

Donatella led him to the office in the corner and

knocked. Browning pulled her eyes away from the monitor and regarded her guest. She stood and came right over.

"Agent Dabria, won't you and Detective Sampson please come in and take a seat?" As they entered, she extended a hand to Sampson. "Detective, I'm Agent H.E. Browning. It certainly is a pleasure to finally meet you," she said with a wide smile.

Donatella couldn't wait to get to the purpose of their visit. "Were you able to ascertain anything from information that's been provided?"

Browning rolled her eyes in mock displeasure. "Always straight down to business," she said, returning to her seat. She retrieved the folder that was squared away at the left corner of her desk, opened it, and said, "Yes, our latest unsub."

She fingered the papers until she found what she was searching for and said, "Male in his late twenties to early thirties. The way in which he has orchestrated the abductions and crime scenes suggests he's highly intelligent. His MO seems to be varying. He started off with college coeds, young, blonde, similar stature but varying backgrounds. But he changed completely when it came to Detective Porter. It seemed more personal, almost as if he had something to prove.

"If I had to guess, something from his childhood started him down the path with the first two victims. They didn't necessary pose a challenge for your killer, so he went after someone who did. What better way to prove you're better than the police than to abduct the person who's investigating you?"

She closed the file. "That's all I have for now. Give me some more time and any additional information, and I'll be able to refine my profile." She reached across her desk with the file extended in the direction of Donatella, who grabbed it and stood.

"Thank you once again for your assistance. We look forward to your refined analysis posthaste."

"Sure thing, Agent Dabria," she said, leaning back in her chair. "Detective, it was a pleasure meeting you."

Back at their vehicles, Donatella said, "I have a few stops to make, but let's plan to connect later this afternoon. In the meantime, I think it would be prudent to start looking at the case from the beginning to see if anything sticks out that may have been overlooked."

"I'll grab my case file from HQ. Call me when you're free," he said.

They both retired to their vehicles and drove away. In her car, Donatella couldn't help but wonder about the change in the assailant's MO and if it was a harbinger of things to come.

THE UNSUB SAT in a gray Honda Accord Sport watching the front door. The standard automobile color changed every couple of decades, and it just so happened that gray was the "it" color now. He purchased this vehicle for one simple reason, to blend in. The additional acceleration could also come in handy if he encountered a touchy situation. He did however need to make a minor alteration, tinting the windows to thirty-five percent, the maximum amount allowed in North Carolina. He didn't want to be easily identified should an incident occur.

He'd watched his quarry the last couple of days and

thus far managed to stay invisible. And he expected today would be no different. He looked to the dash. *8:15, running a tad bit late today,* he thought. Today was Troy's day off from his profession, so he had plenty of time to kill.

The target's blonde neighbor struggled out the door with both hands full and a freckle-faced little girl pulling at her shirttails urging her to move quickly. She struggled to fit the key into the lock and shooed away the little girl so she could focus. After several more attempts, she managed to slide the key into the lock and secured the home. As she turned to head toward her car, she stumbled into her daughter. To catch her balance and to keep the toddler upright, she dropped the load she was carrying in her arms.

As if on cue, a do-gooder on his early morning run noticed the trouble she was having and jogged up to her door to lend a hand. Within the span of thirty seconds, all her belongings were recovered, and the good Samaritan helped her to her car. He watched as the runner received a grateful hug from the mom, and when she turned to step up into the SUV, the runner took a discrete look at her butt with a smile on his face.

The fury in the watching assailant began to build, not because of the man looking at her ass but because of what the woman represented. The rage brought back feelings he suppressed from his childhood, how his mom would don a blonde wig when stopped by the police. In nearly every situation, the officer would let her off with a warning, and on the rare occasion when that didn't work, she would wear the wig to contest the ticket. In every situation, she was let off from the ticket, saving her points on her license and only needing to pay the court cost.

He recalled a particular situation when his mom was

stopped by the police and went through her normal act. Again, the officer let her off with a warning. She turned to Troy and said, "It's important you learn how to deal with people to get what you need from them. Men are more inclined to react favorably to a blonde batting her long, lush eyelashes at him than a brunette."

The turning point came while he was in high school and he walked in on his mom and the superintended in the dilapidated building they lived in. It was another month in which they were short on rent, and when he saw her in that blonde wig and him on top of her...

The door he'd been watching finally opened, and out walked Detective Sampson looking worse for wear. He hadn't even looked in the watcher's direction before falling into the driver's seat and starting up his vehicle.

He followed Sampson, who deviated from his route of the last few days. When he pulled into the Starbucks drive-thru, he circled the building and parked between a black VW and a gray Jeep. The stop took five minutes, and then they were back on the road.

Although he had not been in this particular section of town, he knew they were just outside of the Uptown area. Sampson pulled into an open parking lot, and the unsub was surprised when Sampson turned his car into an open space next to where Special Agent Donatella Dabria was parked and standing outside of her vehicle.

He watched as the two had a brief conversation before walking into the building. The voice in his head said, *It's time to find new prey.* An involuntary twitch brought a momentary smile to his face.

4

"Just look at him, Marcellous," Jasmyn said, tilting her head in the direction of the family room. "He loves spending time with his god-mommy. I'm so happy she agreed to such an important role considering all the turmoil she was going through at the time."

"I agree, babe. And I think it's been good for her as well. I'm sure she encounters her fair share of miscreants on a daily basis, and having an opportunity to unwind with a kid who doesn't have a care in the world has to brighten her day."

Jasmyn kissed Marcellous on the cheek and set her head on his shoulder. "I love you, Marcellous Thompson. We made a beautiful little human. We should probably make another one."

"Well, um," he stammered, "I've not thought about it. I…"

The doorbell rang, and Marcellous was quick to say, "I'll get it."

"Saved by the bell yet again, Mr. Thompson. But we will

continue this conversation," she said, sitting up so he could go answer the door.

As he rushed to the foyer, she walked over to the refrigerator to grab a water bottle.

"What an unexpected surprise," he said. "Come on in. Jasmyn's in the kitchen, and Donatella's in the family room with Sebastian."

Seconds later, Marcellous entered the room with Sal and Jane following closely behind. Jasmyn rushed over to Jane. "I didn't know you guys were back," she said, embracing the older woman in a hug.

"We arrived late last night but wanted to stop by this morning to say hello."

"Well, I'm glad you did. You must tell me all about the trip, and I hope you took pictures."

"Tons of them," Jane said as Jasmyn led her to the family room.

Donatella stood from her seated position on the floor, and Sebastian struggled to follow suit. After two tries, he was steady on his feet and ran over to grab Jasmyn by the leg.

"Jane, welcome back," Donatella said, hugging Jane and then turning to hug Sal as he and Marcellous entered.

Jasmyn turned to greet Sal. "You're looking great! Been working out on vacation?"

He smiled sheepishly and in his gruff New York accent said, "Whatcha trying to say, that I was fat before?"

She laughed as he kissed her on the cheek. "Not at all, Sal."

"At 5:00 a.m., he was running on the beach. Then in the afternoon, instead of sitting in the sand, enjoying the atmosphere with his lovely wife, he was swimming in the ocean. The only thing that got him out of the water was the threat of sharks."

"Hey, it gave you an opportunity to plow through the book you were reading."

"It wasn't just any book; it was Marcellous's latest novel, which was great by the way," she said, smiling in Marcellous's direction. "I was sure I had identified the killer, but once again you fooled me."

"Speaking of killers," Sal said, looking in the direction of Donatella, "what's this I hear about the death of a detective?"

All eyes focused in on her direction. "There's not much to tell at this point. From the conversation I had with Detective Sampson, it appears to be the work of the same person who skinned Mandy Cox and Brianna Armstrong."

Sal's brows stitched together. "The same person? That seems to be a big departure from abducting and murdering college girls to abducting and murdering a police detective."

Donatella nodded. "I agree. With this being the third known act by the same individual, we can classify the perpetrator as a serial killer. While the FBI hasn't been officially invited to assist in the case, Sampson, the lead detective, has asked for my assistance, and I have agreed to lend him a hand."

"If anyone can catch him, I know you can," Jane said, interweaving her hand with Sal's.

"Looks like I have a lot to catch up on so I can post an article on my site. Any chance you can give me more insight?" he asked with a devilish grin.

"Sal, you know better," Jane said, squeezing his hand.

"You can't go off asking Donatella for the inside scoop. Plus, we just got home. Let some other reporter handle it."

"Another reporter? Those hacks. The public has the right to know there is a menace stalking the streets, and I've come to be a trusted voice around here. It's my civic duty. I must–"

"Pipe down already," Jane interrupted.

The group laughed at the couple's feistiness, and Jasmyn said, "Switching gears, I bumped into Bethany Evans this morning, and it got me to thinking. It's been a while since we've had a gathering with friends. How about a dinner party in a few days? Marcellous will do the cooking. Donatella, you can bring Detective Sampson if you'd like. It was a pleasure having him here before, and I'm sure he could use a hot meal."

"That sounds like a wonderful idea. While traveling is great, it's nothing like a home cooked meal to say welcome back."

"Plus, it gives you a chance to pump the detective for additional details about the case," Jane said, elbowing him in the side.

"That too."

"Then it's settled, dinner this weekend at our place. I'll send out an invite with the time and menu. It's going to be great!"

The group continued the conversation, Sal and Jane filling them in on their trip. Meanwhile, Donatella hadn't agreed to ask Sampson to be her plus one for dinner, but thought, *It's not a bad idea.*

Now that the deal with Han Zhiwang had been signed, Veronica King advised her assistant, Derrick, that she didn't want to be disturbed for the remainder of the afternoon. She used that time to conduct hours of research on the properties of plant-based chemical compounds.

She found the research to be fascinating and enlightening. She realized that her rudimentary knowledge was that of a novice, and she yearned to learn more. Who knew that tobacco, the world's most beloved plant, was also one of the most toxic? If eaten directly, it could cause a more immediate death.

Then there was the lily of the valley, a sweet-smelling expensive plant that was even featured in the Duchess of Cambridge's wedding bouquet. Another plant that could be deadly if eaten.

While directly ingesting poisons could work, she couldn't count on feeding something to Susan like she'd done to Lydia.

No, those plants wouldn't do, but she did fancy the properties of the rosary pea. Like tobacco and the lily of the valley, ingesting a pea could be fatal. But this plant held a distinct difference. If the head of a needle was coated in the seed paste, a small prick would cause certain death. She filed that one away in her memory bank as her research continued.

The time to obtain the rosary pea could be lengthy, but numerous chemical compounds could be sourced locally. For those she couldn't, she was able to order with guaranteed same-day delivery. *You have to love the internet*, she mused.

At 4:00 p.m., she exited her office. "Derrick, I'm leaving for the day. I'll see you tomorrow."

"Have a wonderful evening, Ms. King."

As she descended in the elevator to the underground parking garage, she figured by the time she rounded up the local products that the ones she ordered would be at her home. She'd still have plenty of time to whip up a batch. *And then the fun begins*, she thought as she drove away.

5

Back in her home at 300 Calgary Lane, Agent Dabria once again pulled out the shoebox of pictures she'd kept from so many years before. This trip down memory lane was precipitated by the delivery of some blue ocean breeze orchids. Keeping them in her house helped create a sense of closeness to her mother. They also brought back the memories of both her mother and father. She allowed her mind to recall the details of a time that was simpler and when the world wasn't as crazy. Lingering an extra heartbeat on the final picture of the three of them, she placed it back with the other and closed the lid. Her attention needed to focus on the mystery at hand.

The investigation started off slowly, like many often did, so she decided to seek reinforcements. After tucking the shoebox back into her closet, she unlocked her phone, located the name she was looking for, and dialed the number. It only took one ring for the call to be answered.

"Agent Dabria," the voice said in a sing-song manner,

"as I live and breathe. How are you doing today? I'm sure you are doing fine. You're always doing fine. But then again, you've called me, and you don't tend to make social calls, so..."

"Bryce, I need your help."

Agitation crept into his voice. "It's BJ." After a moment of silence and realizing the remark would not be acted on, he added, "How can I help you?"

"A few days ago, a CMPD detective was killed in the line of duty. The person responsible for her death is also responsible for the abduction and slaying of Mandy Cox and Brianna Armstrong. Detective Sampson has asked that I consult on the case with him to bring this monster to justice."

"Understood, what do you need from me?"

"Agent Browning has supplied us with an initial profile of the killer. The MO changed slightly with this third death. I need to understand why he went after Detective Porter. I'd like you to pull everything you can about her and send it to me as soon as possible."

"I'm on it."

"Thanks, BJ." Before he could thank her for using his preferred name, she disconnected the call.

While BJ focused on the background related to Detective Porter, Donatella set her eyes on the first two victims.

Mandy Cox was a student at the University of North Carolina Charlotte, and by all accounts her grades were stellar. Hugo Wolfe, one of the creative writing professors, was currently serving time for her murder. According to Sampson, Wolfe was innocent of these charges even though it had been Sampson and Porter who put him away.

Throughout the entirety of his trial, Wolfe maintained his innocence, which was now confirmed to be true.

Donatella set the file down, logged on to her laptop, and accessed the FBI's secured database of currently incarcerated individuals. Utilizing the advanced search option, she entered the parameters she was interested in.

- Name: Wolfe, Hugo
- City: Charlotte
- State: North Carolina

Within seconds, one result was returned. She clicked on the link and found out that Wolfe was serving a life sentence for the death and disfigurement of Mandy Cox. *Doesn't appear his appeal for release has been granted*, she thought, sliding the laptop to the side and retrieving the file.

The second victim, Brianna Armstrong, was a high school senior. She hadn't finalized her college selection, but UNCC had been one of the candidates. After combing through their online profiles and interviews with friends, the detectives concluded there were no obvious intersections between the two girls. Brianna also lived in Raleigh North Carolina, some two plus hours northeast of Charlotte.

Donatella drummed her finger on the desk. *There must be something that ties the girls together. It's just a matter of finding what that is.* Once again, she unlocked her phone, found the name she was looking for, and dialed.

Three rings later, the voice of Detective Sampson came through. "Good evening, Donatella."

"Sampson, I've been reviewing the file you gave me.

Thanks again, by the way. There are a few details I'd like to review in the morning. Can we meet at 8:00 a.m.?"

Her question was greeted with silence. As she was about to confirm if he was still there, he said, "Or we could meet for dinner tonight, and you can ask your questions then."

"Tonight is no good. Tomorrow morning will be fine."

"It's five minutes to seven, and my gut tells me you haven't eaten yet. And you must eat, so why not knock out two birds with one stone?"

Donatella considered the offer before saying, "Sure."

"Great!" he said followed by another moment of dead air. "Let's do Miro Spanish Grille. I'll meet you there in thirty minutes."

"Better make it forty-five," Donatella responded.

An hour later, she walked into the restaurant and surveyed the establishment. The hostess asked, "How many will be dining tonight?"

"I'm meeting someone who I believe is already here."

"Yes, right this way." Donatella followed her deeper into the restaurant where she found Sampson sitting with his back to the door.

"Your guest has arrived," she said. He stood and walked around to Donatella's chair, pulled it out, and helped her into her seat.

"My apologies for being late," Donatella said while unfolding her napkin and placing it on her lap. "An accident on I-485 caused an unexpected delay."

"No worries. It gave me a chance to review the menu," Sampson responded, flashing a smile.

When the waiter arrived, they provided their drink orders and skipped the appetizers. After their drinks arrived, they placed their entrée orders and dove into business.

"In reviewing the file, two things came to mind. Hugo Wolfe was arrested for the murder of Ms. Cox. Did he have any thoughts on who might have set him up for the murder?"

"None whatsoever. Porter and I went back to speak with him, and he couldn't think of anyone. We also paid a visit to his wife, and she couldn't think of anyone either. They were both caught off guard. It might be worthwhile for us to pay him a visit and for you to talk with him."

"I had a similar thought. I suggest we do that in the morning. For now, let's concentrate this conversation on the second victim, Brianna Armstrong. I'm finding it rather difficult to find any points of intersections between her and Ms. Cox."

"Porter and I came to the same conclusion and were still investigating when she was abducted. It might make sense to pay her parents another visit as well to see if we can shake anything else loose."

Donatella nodded as the waiter came back with their meals. After setting the food on their table, he asked, "Is there anything else I can get for you?"

"Not at this moment," Sampson responded. After the waiter departed, he picked the conversation back up, "The thing that really has me stomped is why he went after Porter. My thoughts are that he did it to get at me, to show he can outwit me at every turn. But I feel there has to be more to it than that. And if he did it to get back at me, then where does he go from here? Does he go back to his previous MO, or does he try to stick it to me again?"

"All excellent questions. Once Agent Browning can

delve deeper into his psyche, I'm sure we will have the answers. I've asked BJ to dig deeper into Porter's background. Maybe there is something there that could have drawn the killer to her that we aren't even aware of at this moment."

"Well, I hope one of them finds something soon. I feel like we've been spinning our wheels too long, and I'm sure our killer isn't sitting around. My guess is he's already planning his next attack, and it's imperative we stop him before that happens."

6

Veronica spent the better part of the afternoon experimenting in her basement. The information she consumed from the dark web was more devious than she imagined, at least for how the authors detailed effects of the chemical reactions. She knew that every hypothesis needed a test, and she had a decent idea of how she'd test her concoction.

One of her clients, Patrick O'Donnell, the director of a local YMCA, had come to her as part of the newly formed GIS outreach program. As part of the program, the company partnered with nonprofit organizations in need of updated security. Her team would determine the current weakness within the establishment, design a new state-of-the-art security system, and implement the solution. Employees were allocated charity hours to perform the work, and the systems were all donated free of charge to the nonprofit.

O'Donnell mentioned his Y had been vandalized and looted several times in the preceding months. It seemed no matter how he tried to outsmart the vandals and thieves, they continued to create chaos. What really upset him was he grew up in that neighborhood. His mom worked two jobs to keep food on the table and pay the bills. He would have given anything to have a place like the Y in the neighborhood when he was growing up. Instead, he and his friends ducked the random bullets flying through the streets while they played freeze tag and stickball.

When asked why he continued to reopen, he said, "Because if I give up on these children, who will look out for them?" It was in that moment Veronica knew she would personally oversee the design of his security system and would not sign off on the design until she was completely satisfied.

As Mr. O'Donnell prepared to leave the meeting that day, he turned around and said, "The neighborhood isn't all bad. It's them darn drug dealers, especially Larry Coker and his crew. They sit on the stoop across from the convenience store all day and night slinging that crap. I've called the cops on them several times, and they get rounded up, but by the end of the day they're back out there as if nothing ever happened. I'm pretty sure they are the ones who are doing the damage to my Y as retaliation for turning them in."

"Rest assured, Mr. O'Donnell, what we have in mind will make your location one of the safest places in the city." And for Veronica King, this was not an empty promise. The pain in the middle-aged black man's face touched her heart like nothing she expected. Tonight, she was prepared to pay off on a portion of that promise.

She pulled into the neighborhood and within one minute located the stoop. It was across from the corner store with three men sitting there. She parked her car short of it and finalized her plan of action.

She retrieved the specially designed vial from her bag, being careful not to break it, opened the door, and stepped out of the car. Instead of walking in the direction of the three men, she walked away from them in the direction of absolute darkness.

During their visits to Mr. O'Donnell's Y, she had Derrick drive her around so she could ascertain the lay of the land. As he did, she took notes and knew the direction she was headed led to a dead end.

As expected, she heard the shuffling of feet moving from the stoop. "Larry, look at the ass on that rich bitch," one of the men said. "We've got to get a piece of that!"

She was revolted but smiled nonetheless. *They will certainly get a piece tonight*, she thought as she continued to stroll aimlessly down the street.

They continued to speak in hushed tones as they closed in on her until one of them finally said, "Hey, miss fine thang, why don't you slow down a bit so we can talk."

A second voice rang out, "Me and my boys ain't seen something as fine as you around these parts before. Why don't you let us show you a good time?"

When she felt they were close enough, she repositioned the vial in her hand and turned to face her would-be attackers.

"Wow, sweetheart," the third man said, "you're more stunning up close than you were from a distance. And that dress is wearing every one of your curves just right."

A smile lit up her face, which in turn generated quizzical looks from the three men. In an instant, she threw the vial at their feet and stepped back as the glass shattered and the liquids that had been separated began to mix on the sidewalk. A white vapor began to rise, she took a couple more steps back to ensure she was out of harm's way.

The man closest to her raised his hand and opened his mouth to say something, but the words never came, and the arm immediately froze in place. The other two could sense something was wrong and turned to run away, but it was already too late. One was caught in suspended animation with his right foot partially off the ground while the other was still in mid turn.

As fast as it had started, it had come to an end. She decided she would cross the street and walk back to her car. As she was about to touch down on the parallel sidewalk, she heard the sound of a body hitting the ground and shattering into pieces. A smile crept onto her face as she thought, *I hope you're satisfied with the piece you got.*

As day turned to dusk, the sweltering Charlotte heat cooled by six degrees, and the killer sat unnoticed at the entrance to the Fringe Oaks. The Fringe, as it was called by the locals, had been deemed one of the roughest areas in the queen city, and it fit into his plan perfectly.

In order to carry out f his plan, he'd need some people who were...disposable. He knew his adversaries were well trained and would certainly be motivated. For what he had in mind, he'd need to slow them down enough to ensure the plan would work flawlessly.

A simple cash transaction with a promise of more to come after the job was complete would entice them well enough, even if they weren't aware they wouldn't be around long enough to see the second half of that money. To sweeten the pot, he decided he'd pay for all expenses up front.

It took longer than expected to track down this location, as the killer typically steered clear of the rundown areas in Charlotte, but he knew not to take his safety for granted. He disliked guns, but in this situation he had one tucked against his waist, out of sight of any would-be attacker.

While observing the scene, he identified two locations he'd try his pitch. Three men sat on a stoop near one corner across from a convenience store. About every five to ten minutes, a car would arrive, and one of the men would stand up, walk over to the car, and trade some drugs for cash. When the next car arrived, a different male performed the transactions.

The second location was a house further down the street. From his vantage point, he couldn't discern everything they were doing, but from what he could tell, they had plenty of clients.

He started the engine, shifted the car into drive, and before he could pull off, a voice in his head said, *Wait*. He moved the lever back into the park position and checked the rearview mirrors followed by both side mirrors. Passing by on the driver's side was a pearl-white C-class Mercedes AMG. He immediately understood this car was out of place, so he decided to wait and observe what would happen.

All eyes were on the car as the driver stopped thirty feet from the men sitting on the stoop. After fifteen seconds, the driver's side door opened, and a woman in a white dress exited. She locked the car with her key fob and walked in the opposite direction away from the stoop and deeper into the darkness of the neighborhood.

The eyes of the men on the stoop followed her with each step as they spoke in hushed tones to each other. Deciding on a course of action, all three stood and began pursuit. Their strides were longer and executed with purpose, so it'd only be a matter of time before they tracked her down. Feeling the reassurance of the pistol on his waist, he considered intervening, but he decided this might be a good audition. Sure, it was against a helpless woman, but he could see how well coordinated they were.

He hopped from his car, hurriedly walked the angle that would let him intersect them the quickest, and continued to be vigilant about his own surroundings. He didn't want tunnel vision to turn him into a victim himself.

"Hey, miss fine thang," he heard a voice carrying from their direction. "Why don't you slow down a bit so we can talk?"

A second voice rang out, "Me and my boys ain't seen something as fine as you around these parts before. Why don't you let us show you a good time?"

The attackers closed to within twenty feet of the woman when she stopped walking and turned around to face them.

"Wow, sweetheart," the third man said, "you're more stunning up close than you were from a distance. And that dress is wearing every one of your curves just right."

They closed to within ten feet when he saw a quick motion from the woman and heard glass break directly in front of the men. She backed up several paces as white smoke began to appear in front of them. One of the would-be pursuers raised his hand in the direction of the woman, and then it froze in place.

The killer watched as the other two men were caught in suspended animation as they were turning to run. One of them had managed to lift the heel of his right foot off the ground before he was stopped in his tracks.

His brain couldn't compute what was transpiring until he turned his attention to the woman in the white dress. Her face was a mask of morbid curiosity, and it donned on him that he'd seen her before. She stood in complete silence as the white smoke disappeared as quickly as it had come.

The woman crossed the street, a look of calculated satisfaction on her face, and proceeded back in the direction of her car. She'd only reached the other sidewalk when the man who was suspended in a half-running position tilted forward, crashed to the ground, and shattered into pieces.

The killer began to backtrack to his car, realizing the woman never even looked back as the guy hit the ground. *What the hell was that?* he asked himself as he rushed back to his car. *I don't know what it was, but I want some, and I know exactly who to call to secure it.*

7

"Come on, class, one more hill to climb! Who's gonna beat me to the summit?"

The collective cycling classes kicked it into another gear.

"Looks like we have a two-way race until the clock expires. Donatella takes the lead with Jasmyn hot on her heels. Thirty seconds to go!"

Jasmyn was panting searching for one more gear to pull from her legs. She spun the resistance once again, now at seventy percent, and pushed her legs to spin a few revolutions faster. She looked to her left and noticed that Donatella was pumping her legs just as fast, but she hardly seemed to be exerting herself. The FBI agent looked graceful with each stroke and didn't look any worse for wear.

"Jasmyn's snaked ahead with fifteen ticks left on the clock. Come on, class, give me all you've got." The instructor counted them down while everyone pushed toward the finish. When he reached zero, he said, "We have a tie! Congratulations, Jasmyn and Donatella. Excellent work, class. See you tomorrow!"

Jasmyn unclipped and walked over to Donatella. "A tie? That's the third ride in a row. I smell something fishy going on."

Donatella grabbed her water bottle and took a swig. "Why, whatever do you mean?"

"I know when I'm being had. You could have easily won that race. While my legs are barely holding my body up, you look like you could ride for another hour. Maybe two."

"Have you ever considered that you could be getting better?"

They walked to the exit and pushed their way through the door, "Listen here. Next class, don't hold anything back. I only want to win when you're giving it your all."

"Giving what your all?" a voice rang out.

The two women turned to find Detective Sampson sitting on the bench outside of the room. Jasmyn detoured in his direction and gave him a hug.

"Apologies for the sweat," she said, stepping back.

"Detective, what are you doing here?" Donatella asked, giving him a piercing glare with those hazelnut brown eyes.

"Coming to meet you for our trip."

"And how exactly did you find me?"

"Give me some credit. I am a detective. We never settled on where we would meet this morning, so I figured I'd meet you here."

Her gaze didn't relent until Jasmyn said while walking away, "Detective Sampson, Donatella has invited you to the dinner party, right?"

"Dinner party, what dinner party?"

Donatella quickly said, "I need to shower. I'll be ready in thirty."

Twenty-nine minutes later, Donatella reappeared in her familiar tailor-fitted black suit jacket with a white blouse underneath and matching pants. Sampson stood on her arrival, and she noticed for all the energy he showcased earlier there was a distinct hint of bags under his eyes and less pep in his step. Telltale signs that his sleep patterns had changed. *Is he burning the candle on both ends determined to solve this case, or is there something else going on?* she wondered as she drew nearer.

"Your car or mine?" he asked once she was standing next to him.

"I'll drive," she said as they began walking in the direction of the exit. She could sense the choppiness in his steps, which wasn't reminiscent of his normal powerful strides. Her car was parked one row from the entrance, since she and Jasmyn normally opted for the earliest spin class with the instructor, Marco. They allowed a passing car to zoom by and then continued to her Audi R8 Spyder. She disengaged the locks and slid into the driver's seat while Sampson hopped into the passenger's.

"How about some coffee?" she suggested, exiting the parking spot.

"That would be great. I had a cup a few hours ago and could certainly use another one.

"We'll stop at Brent's. It's not far from here, and it'll give me a moment to take in some nourishment after the morning ride."

Brent's Coffee Shop on Trade Street had become a staple of Donatella's and was one of the city's many hidden gems. She had been lured there by the psychopath Terri

Buckley when Donatella had been trying to solve the mystery of the children disappearing from Driftwood Springs. Aside from the high-quality drinks and amazing pastries, the atmosphere was subdued, and the staff was friendly. Donatella also liked to visit the location when she needed to think about a case that was giving her fits. This morning's visit would be for the drinks, pastries, and atmosphere. And maybe to dig into what was keeping Sampson awake at night.

The drive from the gym to Brent's took all of five minutes, and Donatella was able to secure a parking spot right on the street. They walked in to the smell of freshly baked goodies and coffee brewing. Although Donatella didn't drink coffee, she could appreciate the aroma from a freshly brewed pot. They proceeded directly to the counter where they were greeted by an enthusiastic barista.

"Good morning to you both. What can I get for you?"

Donatella considered her options. She was weighing between sweet and savory. "I'll have a medium iced chai tea and your bacon and cheese omelet."

"Excellent choices. And for you, sir?"

"I'll take the largest black coffee you have and a cinnamon roll."

"Absolutely."

Sampson handed the perky barista his card and with the transaction complete and his card back in hand, they moved down to the pickup area.

The barista handed them their drinks and Sampson his cinnamon roll. "Please find a seat. We'll bring your omelet out to you."

The early morning rush had not started, so there was plenty of seating available. Donatella normally opted for the oversized chairs when they were available, but today she went for a table near the window so she could speak with Sampson face-to-face.

They took their seats, and Donatella asked, "Is everything okay?"

Sampson was in the middle of taking a drink from his cup, momentarily halted, and then finished. He set the cup on the table. "Everything is fine. Why do you ask?"

"I assure you that everything is not fine. Please give me some credit. I'm an FBI agent. I read people for a living."

She noticed his hesitation and could see the gears working. It was clear something was on his mind, but he was struggling to talk about it.

"Whatever it is, you can tell me. I'm sure it's nothing we can't work out if we put our heads together."

"The message I received while at your house the other night was from Internal Affairs. They called me in to review my actions leading to the death of Porter. In the end, they suspended me for insubordination. They took my shield and my gun."

He was interrupted by the barista dropping Donatella's omelet off. He used this as an opportunity to take a bite of his cinnamon roll, and once the barista had moved on, he continued.

"To make matters worse, the next morning I went to the office to retrieve my files regarding the case and had a run-in with my captain. For some reason, from the moment I came under his command, I've felt he's had some type of grudge against me, but to this day I don't know why. Anyway, he got in my face, words were exchanged, and before I knew it, I'd punched him in the jaw."

Donatella raised a curious eyebrow but didn't interrupt.

"I honestly don't know what happened. I feel there were a few seconds during the exchange when I blacked out, because I don't recall any thought to strike him. It just sort of happened, but I don't regret it."

He paused to take a drink, so Donatella chimed in, "As unfortunate as that may be, it doesn't explain your lack of sleep."

His eyes moved and focused on hers. He shook his head. "You don't miss anything, do you?" He sighed and said, "Since Porter's death, I have had a recurring dream about our ambulance ride when she was pronounced dead before we arrived at the hospital. In it, the medics are doing everything they can to save her, but in the end she still dies. Once she's pronounced dead, I instantly awake and can't go back to sleep."

Donatella reached across the table and placed her hand on his. "What happened to Detective Porter is not your fault. If you continue to let this guilt fester, it will destroy you. It's best you seek help before it's too late."

Sampson nodded. "After last night's episode, I came to the same conclusion. I have an appointment scheduled with the department's psychiatrist for later today."

Donatella smiled. "That's a good first step. I'm sure they will be able to help you navigate what's going on in your mind. And you always have me as a secondary source if you need to chat."

"Thank you, I may take you up on that."

"As for this business with your captain and your suspension, don't let it worry you. I've broken more departmental rules than I can count. Shield or no shield, we're in this together, and we have a killer to find. Let's focus our energy there, agreed?"

Sampson donned a genuine smile. "Agreed."

MEANWHILE ON THE opposite side of town, Veronica King exited the Ballantyne Country Club. Back in her car, she phoned her assistant. "Derrick, I'm on my way into the office. I should be there in about thirty minutes. Please rearrange my calendar accordingly."

"Yes, Ms. King. And how was your breakfast meeting?"

The night before, after returning from dispatching of the hoodlums in the Fringe Oaks neighborhood, she had an unexpected visitor. The intruder startled her after diving under her closing garage door and rolling to a stand.

She surveyed her surroundings and made a mental note she needed to strategically place tools she could use to defend herself. Not only in the garage but around the entire house. The only caveat was that she needed to ensure her daughter, Gina, could not access them. But for the moment, she was caught flat footed and decided her best course of action was the hear the intruder out.

It turned out that he'd witness the incident from earlier and wanted an opportunity to work with her. She remained calm and agreed to meet the man in the morning. She instructed him to leave the garage through the service entrance instead of opening it again for his retreat. Upon his departure, she retrieved the fingerprint dusting kit from the shelf in the garage. She received it as a gag gift several years ago and figured it would never be used. Now as she opened it to reveal its contents, she was hoping it was still good.

After dusting the handle and shining a light on the

dusted area, she revealed what looked to be a full thumb print and a partial forefinger print. She made a call to Molly Jenkins, The Syndicate's technical expert.

"Yes, Ms. King," she said, answering the call.

"I need to have a forensics team sent to my house. I had an intruder and managed to obtain a fingerprint once he left. I'd like to identify who it was."

"Ms. King," Molly said, voice tinged with a faint laugh. "If you take a hi-res photo of the fingerprint and text it to me, I can pull the details on the intruder. No need to send the techs."

Veronica could sense sarcasm in her voice but decided to let it go. She needed details on the intruder before morning, so this evening she would play ball with the spoiled brat.

She disconnected the call and set the camera to the highest resolution she could find. After snapping the picture, she couldn't believe how detailed it had come out. She fired the picture over to Molly and proceeded to wait.

Ten minutes later while sitting on her sofa drinking a glass of wine, she received a text from Molly. "Check your inbox."

She replied with her thanks and opened her laptop. The new message from Molly had an attachment. She clicked on it, and there in front of her was a picture of the man who'd been in her garage. "I've got you now, you bastard," she said as she read through the contents.

Fifteen minutes later, she'd finished reading the file cover to cover, and ten minutes after that she had a plan on how she would handle him. It amused her how much power she had at her fingertips. In less than an hour, she went from not knowing who broke into her home, her sanctuary, to knowing where this man had eaten lunch that afternoon.

She would meet him for breakfast as she promised but couldn't wait to see the look on his face once he realized the tables had been turned.

"It went well. Nothing I wasn't prepared for," she said to Derrick as she started her car, answering his question.

"Excellent. We'll see you soon," he replied and disconnected the call.

8

Jessica Lawson, the special agent in charge of the Charlotte field office, sat at the head of the table in the conference room at FBI headquarters listening to the debrief from Special Agent Cole Vernon. His team, which was comprised of two fresh faces, Maryanne Atwood and Colby Jamison, had been asked to infiltrate a terrorist cell in the city that had smuggled in a dirty bomb.

This had been a role tailor made for Agent Atwood. By all accounts, she was vanilla. You'd see her walking by, and within a blink of an eye your mind wouldn't recall seeing her at all. This allowed her to blend in with any group, and it didn't hurt she spoke five different languages. Her job had been to cozy up with Parker Demes, a college student turned radical. He was second in command of the cell, and once she was in, she began passing data back to Agent Jamison.

Jamison, the know-it-all frat boy, had the propensity to piss off his colleagues, especially Agent Atwood. But the bureau tolerated his antics because he possessed a trait rarely found – a photographic memory. His ability to recall a scene, both visually and orally in perfect detail, had been something the agency couldn't pass up. Once Atwood finished passing along the details to Jamison, he relayed them to Agent Rudolph, the newly appointed IT Director.

With the information that the team in field was able to extract, Rudolph was able to pinpoint the location of the explosive, retrieve it before the terrorist could use it, and arrest every member of the cell before they even knew what hit them.

Once every member of the team completed their after-action report, Lawson said, "Well done, though I'd expect nothing less from this team." She said this with a wry smile because the true nature of their mission went off without a hitch as well.

The official report would be that the cell never had a bomb. The charges for suspected terrorism would stick because they were planning an attack, and Atwood was able to secure the necessary proof that would fry each of them. The bomb had safely made it to an undisclosed Syndicate base of operations. No one outside of the five people who sat in this room knew their cover story was that they worked for the FBI. In reality, they all worked for The Syndicate well before any of them were ever recruited into the agency.

"Now," Lawson said, taking the floor, "I have your next assignment." She passed around folders one by one to each person situated at the table.

"This will be a surveillance assignment with no interaction. While I highly doubt the subject would notice she's being watched, we don't want to run the risk that she figures it out."

"What did she do?" Jamison asked, opening his copy.

"The what is not important. The important thing is you catalog her actions and report back. Every place she goes, every person she meets, take pictures and record times."

"How long are we watching her?" Atwood asked.

"A couple of weeks. Maybe more."

The two operatives glanced at one another but said nothing.

As if she had read their thoughts, she said, "We will be providing you some bodies to aide with the surveillance, but remember that you are responsible for this task." She looked in the direction of Special Agent Vernon. "The bodies we provide you with are to be used at your disposal to do what you advise. Their failure is your failure, and anything other than success will not be tolerated."

"I'd expect it no other way," Vernon said, flipping through his dossier. "Is there anything particular we should be watching for?"

Lawson pondered the question. She had not been authorized to read the team in on the true purpose of the mission, but she'd known Agent Vernon long enough that she couldn't feed him a line like she could the others. His gaze aimed back in her direction confirmed this assertion. She carefully selected her words and responded, "Her motives as of late don't appear honorable, and deceit in any form must be dealt with by any means necessary."

Vernon nodded. "We will not let you down."

Lawson turned to address the IT Director, Agent Rudolph, "Be sure to contact Molly. The folks in R&D have been working on some new tech that may be useful as part of this mission. She's already expecting your call."

"Will do," he said, closing his folder after perusing the

final page. "I'll connect with her right after this meeting. I've been dying to see what the boys in the lab have been cooking up."

"Are there any additional questions?" she asked, glancing at each person sitting around the table. Hearing nothing but silence, she dismissed the group from the room. She couldn't help but feel a sense of pride. She assembled this team, and they flawlessly executed their first true mission for The Syndicate. She could already feel her stock rising. And now that Susan had given the green light to watch Veronica King, she could imagine it rising even higher.

She pulled her phone from her pocket and placed a call. Susan Yates picked up after the fourth ring. "Hello, Jessica. What do you have for me?"

Susan was always straight to the point and preferred directness. "The team has been given the directive to surveil King."

"Any issues with the command?"

"None whatsoever." She saw this as a chance to pump up her team and decided to take it. "Vernon understands the stakes and is keen to follow directions. He has a good sense of when to ask questions and when to fall in line and follow orders. He's managed to harness the strengths of his team for optimal results."

When she stopped talking, there was silence from the other end. *Did I say too much?* she wondered as the silence grew longer.

When she was preparing to say something else to ensure the call had not been disconnected, Susan spoke, "Report to me when you have something. Keep up the good work."

"Yes, ma'am," she said before disconnecting the call. She placed the phone back into her pocket and said to herself, "It's only a matter of time before I have my seat at the table."

THE RIDE to Albemarle Correctional Institution was relatively uneventful. The conversation between Donatella and Sampson veered into the mundane small talk that was present when there wasn't much to discuss.

Donatella had shifted her focus to interviewing Hugo Wolfe. Sampson's notes on his interactions with the wrongly incarcerated inmate were thorough. But she'd discovered a few lines of questioning that she would like to explore. Donatella considered the disposition of the inmate. As he continued to sit in the jail, his innocence all but proven, how helpful would he be. She never understood how the hands of justice could work so quickly to put a man behind bars but ground to a halt when it came time to release an innocent man.

For Sampson's part, he seemed to internalize the conversation they had at Brent's, and she felt he appreciated the advice. Outside of introductions, he'd already agreed to allow her to lead the questioning. In most interactions between the FBI and the local police department, wars of jurisdiction vaulted in front of solid investigative law enforcement work. But with Sampson, it had been different. His goal, his only aim, was to bring this suspect to justice by any means. He didn't need the credit—he needed him off the street.

When she pulled through the gates, she parked in a

spot designated for law enforcement. Upon opening the driver's side door, a rush of hot air displaced the cold air of the cabin. She slid from the seat into the sweltering heat as Sampson did the same.

Sampson took up the lead as they proceeded toward the entrance. There, they were greeted by a corrections officer manning the desk.

"How can I help you?" the ruddy faced officer asked.

Donatella opened her wallet, displaying her badge and identification. "Agent Donatella Dabria and Detective Carl Sampson here to see prisoner Hugo Wolfe."

He studied her credentials and then studied her. He pointed in the direction of the clipboard, and Donatella couldn't help but notice the bend at the tip of his forefinger when he did. "Sign in, and once you're done, please proceed to the metal detectors. If you're carrying your firearm, we ask that you store it in the lockers. You can retrieve them prior to leaving."

Since Sampson was closer to the clipboard, he signed his name first, and Donatella followed suit. They both removed their guns, set them on the tray, and walked through the metal detectors. Another officer watched as they gathered their guns and escorted them to the lockers. They placed both weapons in the same rectangular locker, Donatella placing the key in her pocket.

Satisfied that they complied with the rules, the officer led them deeper into the facility. The walls were center block gray and had a strong smell of lemon and disinfectant. The combination didn't produce a pleasant smell but achieved the cleanliness it was meant for.

They approached a set of doors that required activation from someone watching on the closed-circuit feed. The first door opened, and all three entered. Donatella noticed the light above the door in front of them was red. Sampson was the last one through the first door, and once they were all situated, the door behind them closed and locked.

Five seconds later, the light she noticed earlier transitioned from red to green, and the lock disengaged. The trio exited what Donatella thought of as "the kill box" and continued down the corridor.

They approached a T junction, where the officer lead them to the right. There they found a number of private interview rooms and entered the second one on the left.

"The prisoner will be here shortly," the officer said as he backed out the room and closed the door. Donatella was the first to sit down, taking the chair furthest from the door. Sampson situated himself in the remaining visitor's chair right as the door across from them opened.

Donatella hadn't met Hugo in person and hardly could recall his picture from the papers. Nonetheless, when he walked in, he wasn't what she expected.

His face looked emaciated, and from the way his clothing draped from his body, she wouldn't be surprised if the rest of him looked similar. His hair looked as if it was coming out in patches, and what was left was a stringy gray with no volume. Although he appeared frail, he strode with strength.

He was led to his chair and his shackles were attached to the metal eye on the table. He studied Donatella with his hollow gray eyes before turning his attention to Sampson. "When they said I had a visitor, I hoped it was my lawyer coming to inform me that I was finally free to leave, but here you sit, dashing my dreams yet again. When the hell are you people going to get me out of here?" He pointed his finger at Sampson, causing the chains to rattle. "You know damn well I didn't kill that girl, yet I continue to rot in here."

Donatella interrupted, "Mr. Wolfe, my name is Special Agent Dabria with the FBI. I've had a chance to review the case with Detective Sampson, and it's my opinion you've been wrongly convicted. I'm pulling strings to expedite your release, and I assure you I will not relent until you have been released." She paused and allowed her comment to hang in the air as she maintained eye contact.

"While we're working on your release, we're also combining our resources to find the person responsible for these young ladies' deaths and that of Detective Porter. I hope you'll be able to help us bring this killer to justice."

He immediately began shaking his head. "I've already told the police everything I know. I've done everything I can do to help, and yet you guys haven't found him, and I'm still here."

"I understand your frustration–"

"No, you don't," he yelled. This elicited movement from the guard, but Donatella raised her hand, signaling them to stay in place. "You don't know what it's like to be in this place with killers who look at you with disgust and malice for what they've heard you were convicted of. You don't know what it's like to watch your back every moment of every day wondering when the next time you'll be confronted, when you'll be –" He dropped his head.

"Mr. Wolfe," she said, lowering her voice to try to calm him, "we've already submitted the request to move you out of gen pop. I suspect this order will be fulfilled today. In fact, after our meeting, you'll head back to your cell only to collect your belongings. While it's not your freedom, it's the first step."

Wolfe studied her and after several seconds nodded. "What do you want to know?"

"You mentioned to Detectives Sampson and Porter that you couldn't think of anyone who would want to cause you harm."

He nodded in agreement.

"You also admitted to having an inappropriate relationship with the victim, Mandy Cox."

Again he nodded and added in a whisper, "Yes, that's correct."

"Is it possible someone found out about the improper relationship you had with a student?"

"I don't think so. We were extremely discrete. Her roommate was unaware of the relationship, and the school never let on that they were aware. Otherwise, I would have been terminated with cause."

"Why, Professor Wolfe, did you engage in a sexual relationship with the victim?"

Even in his current state, Hugo's complexion reddened when faced with the question. "It was her idea. She wasn't a good writer. In fact, she wasn't decent either. When she realized she was growing close to failing the class, she propositioned me with favors for a favor."

"Sex for a better grade," Donatella asked.

"Yes – sex. I wanted to turn her down, but she was attractive, desirable, and willing. The deal was sweetened when she agreed it could continue outside of the current academic term. That's ultimately what caused me to agree with the request."

"Would you say over the course of your relationship

that you had gotten to know the victim outside of just the physical interactions."

"Yeah," he said, "it was rare, but sometimes we would talk afterward. All-in-all, she was a good girl, a sweet girl, and what happened to her should've never happened." He adverted his eyes and focused on the ground.

"Do you think she could have made a similar agreement with other professors?" Donatella asked.

Hugo's head snapped back up and with his eyes full of fire. "No! Never! She wouldn't make the same agreement with anyone else. It was just me."

Donatella and Sampson turned toward one another, passing a knowing glance.

"She wouldn't," he continued, his comment losing steam. "She wouldn't."

9

Donatella sipped her iced green tea while reviewing the day's events and the state of the case. The conversation with Hugo generated a new thread to pull, additional male professors of Mandy Cox. On their departure from the penitentiary, Sampson mentioned he and Porter were preparing to investigate her professors when a fire broke out in the records office. By the time the records became available, the CMPD had their efforts focused on Hugo Wolfe.

She downed another sip when the doorbell rang. She used her phone to view the security feed from her front door, *Sal*. Walking to the door, she wondered what brought him by this late in the evening.

"Hello, Sal," she said, opening the door. "How can I help you?"

"I was driving home from the grocery store and said to myself, 'Sal, it's been way too long since you've paid Donatella a visit.' And being the nice guy that I am, I stopped by Duck Donuts and grabbed a half dozen." He produced the box of donuts. "Not to mention, I brought some milk too." He pulled a half gallon of milk from behind his back.

Her eyes focused in on him like lasers. He quickly added, "I know what you're thinking. You don't eat donuts. Too many calories and too much sugar. But these are handcrafted at the time you order them, so they are always fresh, and they have endless combinations."

He quickly flashed a smile, and she said, "Come on in, Sal."

"Perfect! I'm telling, you these things will change your life."

She led him to the kitchen where she retrieved one glass along with two saucers from the cabinet and tore two paper towels from the holder. Sal opened the box displaying six different donuts from chocolate with nuts and caramel drizzle to lemon with strawberry toppings. She picked one at random and sat on the stool across from him.

"Okay, spill it, Sal. Why are you really here?"

He finished chewing on his bite from the chocolate covered donut and said, "Since you asked, I'm interested about the case that you and Sampson are working on. Care to give me any details on the record?"

"You already know I cannot divulge information regarding an ongoing investigation."

"Okay, but you are able to provide me some details off the record, right?"

When it came to investigating a story, Sal was like a dog with a bone, so Donatella was fully aware he would not let it go. She sighed. "We're looking at the case by starting with the first victim. It's clear the person behind bars, Hugo

Wolfe, is not responsible for her disappearance or her death." She continued by telling him about their visit to speak with Hugo in person, leaving out the nugget about the other professors.

"We're also trying to determine the correlation between victim one and victim two."

"Why not include victim number three, Detective Porter?"

"Our FBI Profiler, Agent H.E. Browning, believes there was a deviation for victim three. She's considering the need for him to seek a more challenging prey. But victims one and two are similar in age and appearance."

"But the first victim was attending college, and the second was only a senior in high school."

Donatella didn't want to let on what she'd been thinking, that the second victim may have been considering the same school in which the first victim attended. But she was sure it wouldn't take long for Sal to come to that same realization.

"You're right, Sal. We still feel there is a stronger correlation between the first two and that the third is an outlier."

Sal eyed her with a curious glance but didn't say what was at the forefront of his mind. Instead, he said, "So if the profile is correct and he was looking for a greater challenge, does he stay at this level, or is he looking to risk more and attempt a greater feat?"

This thought crossed her mind as well, and she knew it was something worth exploring. "At this point, it's too early to tell. We're following this initial thread and want to see what will be uncovered once it's been thoroughly explored."

Before Sal could pepper her with another question, her

phone rang. She pulled it from her pocket and said, "This is Donatella." A moment of silence then, "What can I do for you, Detective?"

Upon hearing the word "detective" and noticing a slight change in her voice, he had a pretty good idea who had called. Being the ever-inquisitive reporter, he turned his attention to the conversation. He could only hear Donatella's side, but he'd eavesdropped on enough conversations that he could accurately fill in the other side.

"Tonight's no good. I'm going over some information with Sal."

Silence

"Breakfast at 7:30 will be fine. And who are these people I need to meet?"

Silence

"Okay, I'll see you then."

When her call was complete and her phone stowed away in her pocket, Sal said, "You know, you could do much worse than Carl. It's clear to everyone he has eyes for you."

"We're colleagues and nothing more. He simply wanted to discuss the case and mentioned he had some friends who were willing to pitch in."

"Believe what you want, missy," he said with a smile while rounding up his belongings. "Good men are hard to come by, and that Detective Sampson seems to be at the top of that list. Anyway, I think I have what I need. Thank you for the hospitality, and I'll be taking the rest of the donuts home with me."

Donatella escorted the grizzled journalist to the door. "Sal, don't you go digging too deep. This killer is not to be trifled with. Just because he's put his female victims on display doesn't mean he hasn't killed men before."

"No need to worry about me. Danger is my middle name."

"That's what I'm afraid of," she said as he walked toward his car. When she shut the door, she thought back to his comments about Sampson and realized that hadn't been completely honest with him or herself. They were indeed colleagues, that was true. But there had been occasions when she realized she cared for him. Maybe a little bit more than friends.

She decided that for the time being she would put those thoughts out of her mind and focus on the case. That was her most pressing concern.

10

There aren't many things in life that Veronica King despised, but there are a few that top the list. Drivers switching into the fast lane without signaling only to drop their speed below the speed limit. Moviegoers talking nonstop during a movie. Cold food that was supposed to be hot and hot food that was supposed to be cold. People who neglected and abused dogs. She firmly believed there was a special corner of hell specifically allocated for them. But most importantly, she despised that cheating son of a bitch she called a husband. *Well, her former husband who is still presumed to have run off with his mistress*, she thought as she walked down the stairs.

The corners of her mouth raised into a grin as she thought about the power she wielded in putting an end to him and her. Of course, her hands were forced, as it was the only way to save her daughter, but that decision led her down the path where she sought more and more power. A thought flickered across her mind recalling it was Terri Buckley who paid the visit to her GIS office that precipitated the course she was currently traveling. Her smile widened with the memories of Buckley continuing to flood her thoughts.

Upon reaching the bottom of the staircase, she turned the corner and headed in the direction of her front door. While she was getting dressed, she heard the paperboy, or in her case the paperman, fling the paper against her door. She could obtain her news digitally but still preferred the feel of the physical paper in her hands. Furthermore, it gave her an opportunity to disconnect from her digital device for a few minutes in the morning.

She opened the door, noting the stifling heat and the humidity in the air, retrieved the newspaper, and ducked back into the comforts of her home. She headed to the kitchen where the smell of freshly roasted French Vanilla Folgers coffee filled the room. She poured a cup, sat down at the island, and opened the paper to the financial section.

Over the last month, she had been her own counsel as she'd been considering taking the company public. Doing so came with pluses and minuses. The major plus would provide an influx of capital, which would allow them to accelerate the R&D for her pet project. However, the biggest minus was the annual financial reporting. While her books were theoretically clean, she'd been forced to stretch the truth on a couple of initiatives that The Syndicate mandated of her. Thus far, it hadn't caused an issue, but she could only imagine the continued request that would come her way. This amplified her need to sit atop of that organization.

A plan was still materializing on how she would achieve this feat. Nonetheless, she knew it wasn't anything she could rush into, nor could she allow her plans to be discovered. During her meeting with Susan, when she witnessed the destruction of the FBI building, it was clear their reach was unlimited. Susan was like any other person. She had to have a weakness. Although The Syndicate did its level best to eliminate leverage points from those at the top of the food chain, there had to be something that could be used against her. King made a mental note to follow this thread further when the time allowed.

In her distracted state, the information she read was simply words stamped on a printed page. She took another drink from her mug and folded over the newspaper. Her phone vibrated next to her, and she absentmindedly answered.

"King."

"Good morning, Veronica," Susan's voice rang out from the other end. "Anything interesting in the paper this morning?"

She resisted the urge to look around, because she had her house routinely swept for bugs and cameras during the cleaning crew's biweekly visit. Nonetheless, she still wanted to know how Susan always knew what was going on inside of her home.

"Nothing of note."

"Oh, I guess you haven't made it to the lifestyle section yet. Anyway, that's not the reason for my call. With the death of Lydia Brooks, there is a vacant board seat. In your email, you'll find the name of the person you need to install in that seat. It's imperative that this is done with no fuss. I've already ensured you have the necessary votes. See to it that this is done within the next two weeks. Time is ticking."

Veronica pulled her phone away from her ear, finding

that the line had been cut. *What did she mean that she'd already secured the necessary votes?* The more the question danced across her mind, the more she realized she probably didn't want to know the answer. One thing for certain was that she didn't appreciate being told what she would do with her company.

Idly, she recalled the other veiled reference about the lifestyle section. Against her better judgment, she searched out the section, curiosity getting the best of her. On the front page was a feel-good story about a local home florist and her amazing plants. Veronica disregarded this as the reason for the reference and quickly turned the page. Page two didn't shed much light either, as the main story was about a Boys Scout troop bagging groceries at the Publix Supermarket on 521. She was prepared to close the paper when an article on page three caught her attention.

Headline: Local Man Continues Cleanup Efforts

YMCA Director Patrick O'Donnell has spent the last three years on a mission to clean up his neighborhood, one considered to be one of the worst in the city because of the rampant crime, drugs, and deterioration. When questioned about the biggest problem facing his community, Mr. O'Donnell didn't mince words.

"It's these drug dealers. They are destroying our community with that stuff. Kids haven't been able to go out a play without the fear of bullets whizzing by. Parents are fearful to simply grocery shop to feed their families. This foolishness has to stop."

Well, it appears that Mr. O'Donnell may have gotten his wish, in a bizarre turn of events. What could only be described as the remains of suspected dealer Larry Coker and his accomplices were found. One in an animated state, the other broken into pieces. Authorities are still baffled by..."

Veronica's mind was racing. *How in the hell could she have tied this to me?* Her anger was building, and all she could see was red. The pressure was building behind her ears, and to relieve it she flung the coffee cup across the room, shattering it against the back door. A distant voice seeped into her consciousness.

"Mommy, is everything okay?"

She turned to find Gina standing behind her rubbing her eyes. She took a deep breath, trying to regulate her breathing. "Yes honey," she said, turning to face her daughter with a smile on her face. "Everything is fine. Mommy just dropped her coffee cup. Why don't you go back upstairs and get dressed for school? I've laid your clothes out on your bed."

"Okay," she said, turning around and heading back upstairs.

Veronica grabbed the broom and dustpan and proceeded to clean the broken glass. As she did, she thought, *Susan must go.*

DONATELLA CONTINUED to sit patiently in her car for the person occupying the parking space to buckle her infant safely in the car seat. She allowed Sampson to pick the breakfast location, and he selected the Original Pancake House in Midtown. This was her first time visiting OPH, as it was known as to the locals, but she'd heard positive reviews. With the little one appropriately secured, the woman waved an unnecessary apologetic wave in the direction of Donatella as she hustled into the driver's seat and immediately pulled out. Donatella backed into the spot and headed into the restaurant.

The décor was simple and what you'd expect to see from a chain brunch spot. Ample seating with tables, booths, and half booths. Pictures and jerseys from local sports teams. A picture of their famed oven-baked apple pancake. Plenty of lighting.

"I'm meeting someone," Donatella said after greeting the hostess. Surveying the seating area, her peripheral vision caught rapid movement from the left. She shifted her focus and noticed Sampson waving her over.

Each man stood when she arrived at the circular booth. "Donatella, allow me to introduce you to a few of my colleagues from the force," Sampson said as he greeted her with a hug. He started by introducing the person furthest away from him.

"Meet Victor Martin, a true marksman with any firearm, and Travis Sanchez a master tactician." Donatella shook Martin's hand followed by Sanchez's.

"If you need to have something blown up or disarmed, Josh Kirby is your man. And RJ is a legacy who doesn't allow the fact that his father, grandfather, and great grandfather were all police officers in Atlanta define who he is."

"Nice to meet you," Kirby said, shaking hands with the FBI agent.

"The pleasure's mine," Donatella responded before shaking hands with RJ.

"Lastly, we have Alfred Smith and Johnathan Torres. You'll be hard pressed to find one without the other, and their combined years of experience on the force are more than all the rest of us put together." Donatella once again shook the proffered hands, and afterward they settled into the booth.

Sampson started, "Thank you for meeting us this morning. As I mentioned the other day because of my actions on the case and my subsequent attack on a superior, I have been suspended from the force."

"The asshole got what he had coming," Kirby interrupted, followed by nods around the table.

Sampson continued, "When Detective Porter went missing, the six men sitting here with us today were tasked to help locate her. When the trail went cold from the hotel, a plan was devised to flush out the suspect and it seemed to have worked. They followed the suspect across state lines into South Carolina, where they were led to a house. The tactical decision was made to enter the house, believing time was of the essence. Unfortunately, it was a trap. Long story short, Sanchez here nearly lost his life. It's truly a miracle he's here with us today. The suspect escaped into a tunnel under the house that led next door. He managed to drive away without anyone giving him a second glance."

"So, you see," Martin picked up, "we have a vested interest in catching this killer. He took one of our own, killed her, and managed to slip through our fingers. We cannot, will not let him get away with it. We will bring him to justice or bring him down. One way or another, this monster will be taken off the streets."

Donatella looked into his eyes and could see the truth in his words. These guys were on a mission, and their resolve was absolute. She turned to Sampson, and sensing the question she was prepared to ask, he quickly interjected.

"This is off the books. They are helping on their own

accord, and it's not being run as an official investigation. The department is still looking for the killer, but none of them are involved. But considering my current situation, they have access that I no longer have, plus they are personally motivated to see this through until the end."

Donatella, who'd become averse to working with a partner after her last one turned out to be a sociopathic killer, found it hard to trust anyone but herself. But she had to admit Sampson was key in saving Jasmyn Thompson when they worked together previously, and if he had trust in these individuals, maybe she could trust them too.

With the knot easing in her stomach, she asked, "What do you have in mind?"

They spent ninety minutes reviewing the information that Donatella and Sampson had collectively gathered to this point and discussing their next steps. They needed a base of operations, and Smith and Torres said they had the perfect place, an old crack house that the department had turned into a safe house some fifteen years ago. Since then, the neighborhood had been cleaned up, and no one remembered it even existed except for them. With that agreed upon and the next steps they'd each take, the group broke up.

As Donatella pull into her garage, she recalled a fire in Sampson's eyes that she hadn't noticed before. As he walked the other detectives through their tasks, he was like a general commanding his troops. He was in full command, and his confidence soared with each passing moment. Stepping out of the car and preparing to close the garage door, she noticed a FedEx delivery truck stop at the foot of her driveway.

The driver hopped out, lifted the rear door, and started

rummaging through the packages. He placed a box on the edge of the truck's rear entrance, jumped down, hefted the box against his chest, and headed in her direction.

"Package for Donatella Dabria," he stated from halfway up the driveway.

She appraised him, concluding he wasn't a threat, but she was skeptical, as she was not expecting a package. And considering the last package she received, she was on guard.

"I'm Donatella," she said, walking out from the garage to meet him in the driveway.

He placed the box at her feet and reached to his hip. Donatella immediately went into defensive mode, prepared to drop him before he could furnish any weapon. Her eyes quickly darted to where his hand was headed and noticed something black hanging from his side that she hadn't noticed before. Her muscled tensed, and he said, "I'll need you to sign for the package." He pulled the signature pad that was connected to his belt.

The tension in her body relaxed, but not before the carrier's eyes connected with hers. Panic and confusion drew over his face as he observed the look on hers. She softened her gaze, smiled and said, "Sure, where do I sign?"

Hand trembling, he handed her the pad, never taking his eyes from her. She took the pad, scribbled her name, handed it back to him, and said, "Thank you. Have a great day."

He yanked the pad from her hands and hurried back to the waiting truck, glancing once over his shoulder to ensure he wasn't being followed. He sped off in a fashion like the driver from her previous delivery.

Donatella looked at the shipping label. No return

address. She was deciding if she should take it into the house and open it, or if she should open it at all. Just then, her phone vibrated in her pocket. She retrieved it and looked at the caller ID to see BJ was on the other end.

"Yes, BJ."

"You're there, and I see my package has arrived," he said in a frantic rush. "I can't wait for you to see the goodies I have in store for you."

"BJ, it's not a good idea to send unknown packages to my home. It could have dire consequences."

He was silent for a moment and then comprehending her meaning said, "You're right. I will alert you next time. In the meantime, let me know when you have opened it up, and I can walk you through your new gear."

Ten minutes later, Donatella was situated in her study with the package she received from BJ and him in a video conference connected to her television.

"Great! It appears the package arrived in one piece. On top there are three tailored black blazers. You can remove all three, but please try one on."

Upon removing the blazers from the box, Donatella recognized the brand as the only one she wears. "BJ, how do you know my designer and my measurements?"

"Please give me some credit. I am a certified genius and a computer whiz. It wasn't a hard mystery to crack."

He waited while she slipped on the new garment.

"You'll notice a few differences. There's an inner button you'll want to fasten before buttoning the outer one. If my math is correct, which I'm sure it is, the inner button will keep the jacket firmly affixed to your body but shouldn't restrict any movement."

As she fastened the button, BJ continued to talk.

"You'll also notice it's roughly one kilogram heavier than your traditional jacket. This was the lightest I could achieve while still guaranteeing the properties of the enhancements."

"And what exactly are the enhancements?" she asked while simultaneously twisting and validating the fit.

"Well, from the technical side, each jacket is equipped with an accelerometer sensor and a gyroscope sensor. Both are used to determine if you are falling from a distance greater than three stories."

Donatella raised an eyebrow, "And how exactly is that a helpful piece of information?"

"If and when a fall of this magnitude is determined, a signal is sent throughout the jacket and a series of gas explosions fire at once, discharging a protective bubble around your body. It should take no more than three-tenths of a second to complete. Plenty of time before you hit the ground."

Donatella computed the math from a four story fall, quickly determining her definition of plenty of time and BJ's definition were not the same. "And what happens if the fall is under three stories?"

"Then I'll sign your body cast once you're released from the hospital. Anyway, moving right along. Next, you'll find my favorite accessory. Please remove the box labeled one."

She did as instructed and opened the box. "Contact lenses? BJ, my vision is perfectly fine."

"Indeed, it is, but these are not prescription. Go ahead and put them on."

Having never worn contact lenses of any kind, it took several tries, but she finally managed to affix them correctly.

"Now these aren't just any contact lenses. They're smart lenses. They've already been paired to the Bluetooth on your phone –"

"BJ, how exactly are they connected to my phone?" When he didn't immediately answer, she said, "You and I are going to have a long talk about boundaries."

"Noted. As I was saying, these are smart lenses. For example, if you know the identity of someone you are tracking, every face you encounter goes through facial recognition. If there is a ninety-percent match, your phone will chime displaying both the image that was taken along with the source image. You can calibrate the match percentage up or down, but studies have shown that ninety percent is the sweet spot.

Coupled along with facial recognition is tracking mode. To activate, you simply blink three times in rapid succession. A holographic target comes into view. Maneuver your head up, down, left, or right until the subject is within the target. Close your eyes for three seconds, and when you open them the target can run all they want, but their individual heat signature will lead you right to them. Now the obvious question is if they alter the heat signature by entering a cold room or getting wet. If your eyes pass through any source they may have gone through, the lenses will calibrate for the temperature and adjust accordingly."

Skeptical, Donatella asked, "And this tech has been proven in the field?"

"It's worked flawlessly in the lab after several iterations, and I'm confident it'll pass any field test." Donatella eyed him, but he continued, "Finally, to the feature that gave me the most trouble. If you slow blink three times you'll activate, wait for it, wait for it… Night vision.

"This feature is on par with any military-grade night vision you can find, and without the range of vision drawbacks. While you won't experience tunnel vision, you'll still have the issue of being blinded should a light come on while you are in night-vision mode.

"To deactivate any feature, simply close your eyes for five seconds, and the smart lenses will reset. It's perfectly okay for you to sleep in these lenses. In fact, I recommend it. You'll want to remove them once a day for no longer than ten minutes to let your eyes breathe. Other than that, you shouldn't encounter any issues."

Donatella, who was preparing to pop the lenses from her eyes, turned her attention to the box and removed the last item. "Am I clear to open this box?"

"Oh, yes. Box number two. Please go ahead."

She opened the lid to find a smart watch tucked inside. BJ continued, "This isn't your ordinary smart watch."

Of course not, Donatella thought and then said, "Let me guess. It's already linked to my phone as well."

"Yes, it is." BJ shook his head to recapture his thought. "But that's not the important part. This device monitors all your vitals. If for any reason it determines you are in distress, it'll administer a dose of adrenaline and a cocktail of antibiotics into your body. While not one-hundred-percent foolproof, hopefully it'll provide the upper hand in the confrontation."

From the look on his face, Donatella surmised the events at the Panthers' stadium continued to weigh heavy on his mind. Although she did everything to reassure him it wasn't his fault, until he believed it wasn't, he would continue to beat himself up. She placed the watch on her wrist and said, "Thank you, BJ, for continuing to ensure my safety."

He nodded in affirmation. "You're welcome. And one more thing. The details I've uncovered about Detective Porter are waiting in your inbox."

Once again, she thanked him, and they ended the call. She made a mental note to check her email, but for now she needed to pay a visit to the FBI office building.

11

"Beth, I'm so happy you could join me for today's outing," Jasmyn said before sipping from her coffee mug.

"Not as much as I am. I absolutely love being a mom. In fact, being a mother is the best thing I've done thus far in my life. But having a grown-up conversation is a refreshing change from the normal routine, not to mention eating a meal while it's still hot." She accentuated the point by biting down on a piece of triangularly sliced sausage, which brought laughter to the table.

Jasmyn continued, "For me, I gain immense pleasure from watching Sebastian explore his world. The way he studies the sounds that are coming from his toys. When he watches Maggie as she plots around the house during the day. The way he rubs his fingers along a newly discovered texture. I wouldn't change that feeling for the world."

Beth raised her nearly empty mimosa glass and said, "To our children, the unconditional loves of our lives."

"I'll drink to that," Jasmyn said, clinking her mug to Beth's glass.

Beth finished off what was left of her drink, scooped up the last bit of her over-easy egg and chicken sausage on to her fork and savored the final bite. She sat back, sighed, and announced, "I'm stuffed."

"Now don't you go calling it quits on me this early. We still have a day full of activities ahead of us."

"Me. Give up this early? Never! I'm going to make the most of this day, because who knows when I'll get to get some me time again. Which reminds me. You never did disclose what's in store for today."

The waitress discreetly dropped the check off at the table and said, "No rush. You'll pay up front."

Jasmyn reached for the check, but Beth was quicker. "Absolutely not. This is my treat. You inviting me on today's mystery adventure is just what I needed."

Jasmyn genuinely smiled and said, "Thank you. As for what else is on tap, we must complete the mundane first. We need to pick up a few items for the dinner party, then we spend the afternoon being pampered, mani pedis and massages at the spa, followed by our hair appointment at Jacques."

"Jacques! Are you serious? It's impossible to get onto his calendar. How on Earth –"

"Let's say he's a huge fan of Marcellous's books. After sweet talking my husband into autographing the series for him and promising him first print editions going forward, I'm now on the exclusive list of priority appointments."

"Get out of here! I've been trying for six months to get on his calendar. I've been thinking of making a change to my hair, as it's been the same since college."

"There's no time like the present," Jasmyn said as she began gathering her belongings. "Speaking of which, if we don't want to be late for any of our planned activities, we better get moving."

Needing no further encouragement, Beth followed her friend to the cashier. The speed of payment processing had been greatly increased with the tap-to-pay method and made easier by having the option to add the tip early in the process. Once the tap was complete, the cashier handed Beth her receipt, and the pair began walking to the door.

Jasmyn led the way, holding the door open for Beth while she fumbled around to place the receipt in her pocketbook. As she stepped through the exit door, preparing to place her pocketbook back into her purse and to thank Jasmyn for holding the door, an unexpected jolt hit her.

The blow spun her 360 degrees before she collapsed to the ground. Her brain was slow to comprehend what had transpired, but it appeared this was not the case for Jasmyn. Her friend began pursuing a man in a full-out sprint. It was then that Beth realized the pocketbook she'd been holding in her hand was gone, along with her purse. She searched around on the ground, and confirming its disappearance, she realized what happened. She did the only thing that came to her mind, "Thief! Somebody stop him!"

Ever since Jasmyn had been kidnapped by Terri Buckley, she'd had the fear of being vulnerable and unable to protect herself. She expressed this concern to Donatella, who agreed she'd teach her some self-defense techniques in addition to some handy offensive attacks.

"The first defense you have is your awareness," Donatella had said at their first lesson. "Be aware of the people around you and your proximity to them, reading their intent and formulating a set of contingency plans should you need to act. When new people enter the room, assess them for danger, categorize them, and subconsciously track those you consider to be a threat. If an uneasy feeling ever starts to creep in, determine if it's best to remove yourself from the situation.

"You need to be aware of your environment. When you are in a building, spot the natural exits. Aside from them, what could become an exit if necessary and how do you make that happen? Are there things in your environment that could cause you harm or inflict harm on a would-be attacker. Whenever possible, position yourself within the environment to give yourself a viewpoint of as much of the room as possible.

"Finally, you need to be aware of yourself. You need to understand what tactics you've learned and how to apply the appropriate one given the situation. If you've done the first two appropriately, you should have considered strengths and weaknesses of your opponent and how to best use the environment to your advantage. Leveraging this knowledge, you devise a plan of action. The most important thing once the plan has been devised – attack. Don't wait. Don't second guess. Seconds can mean the difference between you going home to your family or them visiting your gravesite."

As Jasmyn gave chase to the mugger, she admonished herself for failing part one. She never identified the threat. She never even saw him coming. But she had to put this out of her mind. As she gave chase, she was assessing the assailant with each step he took. *He's light on his feet but runs with an unnatural gate. His legs appear to be moving faster than his brain is processing. Could he be on drugs?*

While it appeared that the thief was at the top of his speed, she knew she was only exerting seventy-five percent of her max and was still gaining on him with each step. Furthermore, she had followed step two of Donatella's lesson.

When arriving at the breakfast location, Jasmyn familiarized herself with the environment. Ingress and egress for both vehicle and foot traffic. Stores that were already open and those that would be opening later. The construction for a 5/3 Bank next to the structure for the restaurant. And in this knowledge, she knew the chase would be ending soon.

While the assailant grew comfortable with the dwindling number of cars located in the direction he was headed, he neglected to understand the road and pedestrian traffic was closed because of construction. In deciding to escape in this direction, he had now boxed himself into a corner.

She watched as he came to a halt and frantically searched for a solution to this problem he hadn't anticipated. Jasmyn stopped about ten yards from him hearing the faint yells for someone to call the police coming from the direction of the restaurant. The thief turned to face her, face ashen, eyes red, and hair plastered to his face. His breathing was labored for the energy he exerted to get her. He took a calming deep breath and hissed in a raspy voice, "Get out of here, you bitch."

Jasmyn continued to assess the situation while devising a plan, "You have something that belongs to a friend of mine."

He looked down at the purse and wallet in his hands. "Seems like it's mine now. And if you want it so bad..." He dropped them both next to him and reached into his pocket, removing an object. The distinguishable sound of a switchblade locking into place filled the silence. "Then why don't you come and take it from me?"

The words from one of her lessons with Donatella came rushing to the forefront of her mind. "As a civilian, carrying weapons on you is not normal, and while you could carry a concealed pistol, I truly don't recommend it. However, that doesn't mean you don't have options. There are articles of clothing you can wear that could easily double as a defensive or an offensive weapon. It's prudent to consider this when selecting your outfit for the day."

Jasmyn quickly calculated her odds of success. Figuring them at greater than eighty percent, she locked in on the plan and executed. She quickly began loosening the belt around her waist that was more for decoration than to hold her outfit in place. The thief gave her a questioning look but didn't say a word.

With the belt removed, her plan hinged on quick decisive action. She wrapped the belt once around her knuckles allowing the buckle to swing freely. Without provocation, she snapped the belt in the direction of the mugger, connecting directly under the chin into his larynx.

The attack caused him to drop his knife, fall to his knees, and clutch his windpipe, gasping for air. Jasmyn knew the damage wasn't permanent, and in roughly five minutes, maybe ten, he'd be talking normally again.

It wasn't until she heard cheering that she realized a crowd had formed behind her. *So much for awareness*, she chided herself. *I really need to do a better job of that.* Two older gentlemen moved swiftly in the direction of the mugger. One picked up the switchblade and quickly closed it, while the other picked up Beth's purse and wallet.

Beth came into view and rushed to hug Jasmyn. "Oh my God. You were wonderful. How... Where... Girl, you've got to teach me some of that."

"Here are your things, ma'am," the second man said, handing over her purse and wallet.

"Oh, thank you. Thank you so much," she said, clutching them like long-lost pearls.

Jasmyn looped her belt, turned to her friend, and said, "We better get moving. We still have a lot on our agenda for the day."

Beth, still shocked by the turn of events, simply said, "Yeah let's do that. And you have some explaining to do."

DONATELLA DIDN'T MAKE regular visits to the FBI Charlotte field office, and when she did, it was typically at the request of her new superior SAIC Jessica Lawson. Today, she decided to make an unscheduled check-in visit with Lawson. Not because it was mandatory to do so but because she wanted to see how the new head of the field office was operating. She was replacing a man who Donatella considered a mentor and someone she could trust. And for what it was now worth, she didn't fully trust Lawson. She couldn't exactly put her finger on it, but there was something about her aura that gave sinister vibes.

When the elevator stopped on the main level, she stepped from the car and proceeded directly to Lawson's office. She walked in a casual manner hoping to minimize onlookers. Nonetheless, her mere presence in the building garnered attention. While some agents stayed focused on her work, she couldn't help but notice each of the new agents handpicked by Lawson recognized her entrance. Two of them looked away and pretended to go back to their work, but as she moved, she noticed a slight shift in their heads or body angle that meant they were covertly watching her. The other didn't attempt to hide it as they simply watched each step until she entered Lawson's office. She mentally filed this away to dissect later.

As Donatella entered, Lawson slowly looked up and quickly tried to hide the shock on her face at the presence of the special agent. "Donatella, it's a pleasure to see you. What brings you in today?"

Not waiting on an invitation to sit, she took the chair directly across from Lawson. "I heard on the news about the death of the police detective, Porter, from the CMPD. I'm curious if they have reached out to us for any assistance in apprehending the person responsible."

Lawson leaned back in her chair. "Nothing has come across my desk asking for assistance. And should it, we would be more than happy to aid their search. Why do you ask?"

"The death of someone in law enforcement is one thing, but to be murdered in the way she was murdered is something completely different. It's clear we are dealing with someone who is unstable at best or viciously psychotic at worst. It's not safe for anyone to be walking the streets with this person on the loose."

Lawson dug her elbows into the armrest and steepled her hands in front of her chest. "Sound logical, but I'm not surprised. SSA John Brewer said you're levelheaded and you make solid judgment calls."

Hearing Brewer's name from her lips grated on Donatella, a feeling she tried to shake. "If they do call," she continued, "I'd like to be considered for the case. My load is light, and unless a crisis hits, I should be free."

Lawson eyed Donatella for a minute while allowing silence to fill the room. She finally said, "Why don't I do you one better? I'll reach out to their chief this afternoon to let him know we are willing to assist should they want our help. I'll convey that you are available and are anxious to bring this ordeal to an end."

"Thank you," Donatella said as she stood. "Please do let me know what the captain says. Until then, I'll bid you adieu." She tipped her head slightly and turned to exit the room. By the time she reached the elevator, she was convinced more than ever that something was amiss. Lawson was too eager to jump at Donatella's suggestion to help the CMPD, which left a lingering question in Donatella's mind, *What doesn't she want me to know?*

Just then, she received a text from Browning. "I have a final profile for you. Meet me in my office."

Donatella sent a text to Sampson. "Browning has a final profile. How soon can you come to her office?"

His response was immediate. "I can be there in twenty." Donatella gave him the thumbs up and responded back to Browning. "I'm upstairs and will be right down. Sampson is twenty minutes out."

After receiving a thumbs-up from Browning, Donatella proceeded down to the appropriate level, curious what Browning prepared to share.

Meanwhile, back in SAIC Lawson's office, each of The Syndicate undercover operatives piled in. Vernon was the first to speak, "Hey boss, what brought Agent Dabria in?"

"She claimed to be here asking about the case of the detective murdered recently, asked if we had been called in to help and offered to aid should the call come. I advised her that I would reach out to the captain to off our assistance."

Atwood, always good at reading between the lines, said, "Claims? Do you think she had an ulterior motive?"

"It's hard to tell with that woman. She truly gives me the willies. I don't know why we haven't been given the green light to erase her from the picture," Lawson said.

"When the directive does come in, I want to be the one to take down the famed Donatella Dabria," Jamison said, holding two fingers formed into a pistol to his lips and blowing the imaginary smoke from it.

"She's taken down her fair share of adversaries, some with skills more highly tuned than yours. She isn't someone to be trifled with or taken lightly," Lawson responded without looking in his direction. "Anyway, how is surveillance going on our subject?"

Vernon took the question, "So far, nothing to report. The last couple of days, she hasn't done anything out of the ordinary. Tonight, we have Atwood and Jamison on her trail. With it being a Friday evening, we're hoping she breaks from her normal routine."

"Excellent. Let me know if you uncover anything of note regardless of the time of day or night. Agent Rudolph, were you able to connect with Molly?"

"Yes. The equipment arrived yesterday, and I've already completed the installation process. We are going through a few configuration settings. We should be fully operational within the hour."

"It seems you all have everything in order. If anything

changes or you need my assistance, don't hesitate to reach out. The four of you were personally selected, and we have high expectations of you and great plans for you. Don't let me down."

"Not even in our vocabulary," Jamison said, attempting to save face from earlier.

Lawson dismissed the group and pondered, *What game are you playing, Donatella?*

SAL FELT himself getting back into a routine after the lavish trip he spent with his beautiful bride. He woke up at 5:00 a.m. to complete his morning run. Instead of his traditional five-mile run, he cut it down to three miles. For the remainder of his time, he worked out with the dumbbell set he purchased from Amazon and did a set of crunches to finish out the morning. The long hot shower had turned into a sanctuary of its own and helped him to focus his mind for the day. As he dressed, he looked over at his sleeping wife and marveled at how radiant Jane looked.

There were many things he was still getting used to about being a married man. While he preferred to sit at his dinette to work on his articles, Jane instituted a "no work at the table" policy. So he'd been relegated to a small office desk that held his laptop and a monitor. The chair Jane bought him wasn't as comfortable as his old chair with the missing wood pieces, but he had to admit the chair and desk combination was more uniform. And his back didn't hurt after working a full day like it had done many times in the past.

She had also continued on him about his diet. When

she first broached the subject, his mind flashed to rice cakes, soy milk, and an array of impossible meats. But he was pleasantly surprised with the varieties of dishes she'd introduced and the layers of flavor they packed. Not to mention, his clothes were fitting better, and the pouch he'd been struggling to remove was disappearing more and more each week.

As he prepared to leave the room, he contemplated heading to her side of the bed and giving her a kiss, but he decided he would allow her to rest. As he prepared to open the door, her sleepy voice called out to him.

"Good morning, hon. Would you like some breakfast?"

"No, sweetheart," he said, turning around and walking back over to her, "I'll brew me a cup of coffee and find something. You get some rest." He leaned over, kissed her forehead, and proceeded to the door.

In the kitchenette, he dropped a Starbucks K-Cup in the Keurig, placed the mug in the proper location, and started the brewing process. He walked over to his desk, fired up the laptop, turned on the monitor, and opened the curtain. By the time he completed this task, the coffee machine began to gurgle. He returned to the kitchen to grab his mug and shifted his thoughts to the research he needed to undertake.

Donatella hadn't been forthcoming regarding the status of the investigation into the deaths of Mandy Cox and Brianna Armstrong, the first and second victims. She'd been even more tight lipped about Detective Elise Porter, so it was up to him to find the story the old fashion way.

He slid open the desk drawer and retrieved his well-worn mead notebook and overly chewed pen. He scrawled across the top of a new page, "Why the first victim?" He felt the answer to this question would be easier if he understood more about her.

The inappropriate relationship she had with her professor, Hugo Wolfe, had been well chronicled throughout his trial. Prosecutors touted this as his motive for killing her. All along, Wolfe continued to proclaim his innocence, yet that didn't stop a jury of his peers from finding him guilty. But with hindsight being 20/20 and the subsequent murders, his guilt had severely come into question.

Underneath the first statement on his notepad, he added a second question, "Why frame Hugo Wolfe?" He interlocked his fingers above his head and leaned back in the chair, staring at the questions on the paper.

It was clear to Sal that the killer had crossed paths with both Cox and Wolfe. Furthermore, the killer had to know both to set Wolfe up so expertly and for Cox to be taken without a struggle. Sal subconsciously placed the pen in his mouth and continued to think. A thought flickered across his mind, and he lost it as quickly as it had come. The more he tried to bring the thought back to the forefront, the further it drifted away.

Focus, Sal, he told himself. *Stick to understanding Mandy.* As he prepared to dig into the articles about her, he heard the bedroom door open. He turned to see Jane wrapped in her robe headed to the kitchen.

"What are you doing up?" he asked.

"Fixing some breakfast," she replied, opening the refrigerator and removing the cage-free eggs and chicken sausage. "Let's face it. You're about to get bogged down in your work, and when you get hungry, you'll be too distracted and make a bad decision. I'm saving you from doing something that you'll later regret."

Sal smiled, and as much as he wanted to dispute her claim, he knew she was speaking the truth. "You're too good to me," he simply said in response.

"I know. So what are you working on?" she asked, cracking the first egg, setting the yolk to the side, and placing the white into the bowl. She followed up by cracking the second egg, dropping both the white and the yolk into the bowl. Then she seasoned them with a pinch of kosher salt, pepper, and a dash of unsweetened almond milk. She beat the eggs as Sal spoke.

"I'm working on an article detailing the serial killer that Donatella is hunting. Well, unofficially hunting. I figured the answers lie in understanding why the killer selected the first victim, then unfortunately my mind went on a tangent about the professor who was framed and why it was pinned on him."

Jane, a phenomenal journalist in her own right, said, "That makes sense and certainly a good thread to pull. From what I recall from the trial, the victim made herself available to the professor in exchange for him altering her grade. Their relationship –"

The fleeting thought Sal had earlier was beginning to rekindle. He closed his eyes to focus and pull it to the forefront. With a gleeful outburst, he exclaimed, "Jane, you are a genius."

The statement stopped her in her tracks, and Sal continued, "It's all about the access."

"I'm not following," she said, now fully turned in his direction trying to follow his logic.

"In order for Mandy to disappear without causing a

scene, it means she had to know the killer. For the killer to do the frame job on the professor means he had to know him too. But it was the video that continued to throw me off. How did the killer manage to obtain the video to send to the police? He had access to the professor's office. That means he had to have access to the building. Don't you see? Knowing the victim, the professor, and having access leads down one certain conclusion. The killer is likely a professor or administrator at the school."

Jane pondered this statement and said, "You know, you might be on to something. But how will you prove it?"

"Like I always do. Good old, hard-nosed investigations."

Jane frowned at this thought, because the first time he became involved in a Donatella case, he nearly lost his life. Resolute in her decision she said, "Well, if you are determined to follow this path, then I'm going to help you with the investigation. Who knows, we may share the byline after breaking the case wide open."

Sal was taken aback by the comment. For years, he and Jane were on opposite sides trying to get the scoop. And now he was writing only online, and she wasn't writing for anyone. She was a brilliant journalist and was as dedicated to getting the story as he was.

He finally said, "Pull up a chair and let's get started."

12

"Special Agent Dabria, Detective Sampson, thank you both for making time to meet with me," Agent Browning said. "I've spent an enormous amount of time dissecting your unsub. Aside from trying to predict his patterns and what may come next, I try to determine his motivation and history."

She paused and looked at each of them in turn to ensure they were still following. Confident she hadn't lost them, she continued, "From my initial assessment, I'm confident the assailant is a professional male in his late twenties. Skinning his first two victims signifies a true disdain for them or what they represent. I take it you still haven't been able to find an intersection between the victims other than their unfortunate interaction with him."

"Correct," Donatella offered.

"In that case, I'm inclined to say it was something personal about them he didn't like. Given the age discrepancy between the two victims and that of the unsub, it's highly unlikely he had any meaningful interaction with the second victim before her abduction. Given this, I'd surmise the personal thing he didn't like about them involved the way they look. The skinning was a physical manifestation of him de-beautifying them.

"This act tells me there was something in his childhood that had a profound negative impact on his life with women or a woman who looks like the victims. Killing them is getting back at the subject of his hatred."

"The next question we must answer is why Detective Porter was next."

Again, Browning checked to ensure they were still tracking what she was saying. Sampson shifted in his chair, attentive. They were with her.

"While the first killings were a form of payback, the abduction and killing of Porter had a different motive. He brazenly went after her in a public place. While the first two were done covertly, the abduction of Porter was the opposite. Even the method in which he dispatched of her was completely different. She didn't exhibit any of the same physical characteristics of the first two, neither was she skinned like them. This leads to one of two conclusions.

"You are dealing with two different killers who are feeding off one another, both getting the opportunity to exercise their demons utilizing their own methods. They are in essence working together with the ability for both to hide in plain sight."

"But," Donatella interrupted, "you don't believe this to be the case."

"You're correct. I don't. For them to be this well coordinated and to avoid slipping up, they would have needed to be at this for years. And the death of the first victim doesn't support this assertion."

"So what's the second conclusion?" Sampson asked.

"The second and more likely conclusion is that you are dealing with someone who is having a psychiatric mental break, and a second personality is fighting its way to the forefront. The second personality doesn't care about the righteous reasons the primary has. The second personality has now had the taste for blood, and for him it's all about the hunt."

"Reviewing the death of Detective Porter gives these indications. What better thrill is there to turn the hunter into the prey without them knowing they are being hunted?"

Silence filled the room as she gave them time to digest what she'd stated. Feeling enough time had passed, she continued, "My guess is the second personality is the one now driving the actions to kill, while the primary personality is still driving the day-to-day living. The secondary will continue to push the primary to take more risks and go after a bigger score. And at some point, the secondary will begin to drive both the day-to-day living and the hunt.

"To wrap this up with a fine bow. You're looking for a white collar, late-twenties male. Extremely intelligent, makes friends easily, and has normal relationships. He could be married and may have a family. He may suggest he's had memory gaps, losing a portion of a day from ten minutes to a couple of hours. One more thing to keep in mind. As the struggle for control continues between the primary and the secondary, it's very likely the secondary will win out, as it seems to be the stronger of the two. If and when this happens, you'll see an increase in frequency and boldness from this unsub."

"Thank you, Agent Browning, for your thorough analysis," Donatella said. "I do believe this will be a tremendous help in allowing us to apprehend this individual."

"Yes, thank you," Sampson echoed.

"The pleasure is all mine. Now if you don't mind, I'll walk out with you. I have some work being done at my house today, and the contractor will be arriving within the hour. Give me a few minutes to lock up the place, and I'll head out with you."

Browning took her time meticulously filing away the documents on her desk, and once the task was completed she locked up her office and exited the building with the two law enforcement officers.

"Thank you again for all of your help," Donatella said as she and Sampson headed in the same direction.

"I hope it's enough to help you catch your man," Browning responded as she headed to her car that was parked a couple of rows over.

As they left the lot, each going their separate ways, a black Mercedes coupe fired up its engine and began a soft trail behind one of the vehicles.

VERONICA KING'S level of frustration from this day elicited an unusual comment after losing a contract to a subpar competitor. "Your ineptitude is going to cause me to start drinking." And now. as she sat in Hestia Rooftop downing a dirty martini, she toasted to her own foreshadowing.

Hestia, a trendy new restaurant in the Charlotte area, was known for the killer view of the city. And as breathtaking as the view was on any given day, observing the sunset over the city was the marquee attraction. King consulted her watch, noting the event was to take place in five minutes. She drained the remainder of her drink and signaled to the bartender for another.

She composed a text to the nanny while her drink was being prepared. "Thanks again for staying late." Before she could put her phone away, it buzzed.

"Anytime, Ms. King. I love spending time with Gina. She ate all her food, and we finished up with bath time. I'll read her a couple stories and then tuck her in. You enjoy yourself."

"Thanks, I will," King responded.

The bartender placed her drink on the bar and went off to serve another customer. She picked up the glass and headed to the outdoor seating. There she managed to find a seat with a great view.

"Is this seat taken?" a husky voice asked from behind her as its owner came into view.

"It's a free country," she said, never shifting her eyes from the skyline.

The newcomer sat in the chair adjacent to hers. "I don't think I've seen you around these parts. I'm Trevor."

Veronica, whose sole goal for the evening was to have a few drinks and enjoy the sunset, had become adept at reading people. And it was clear that Trevor was going to be a talkative nuisance who'd destroy her serenity.

Letting him know she wasn't interested would be a prudent course of action. And after doing so he'd likely go harass some other woman. Ignoring him was another option, but he doubtlessly lacked self-awareness and wouldn't get the hint to leave her alone.

She inwardly groaned at the situation, realizing it wasn't this moment eating away at her. Continuing to be under the thumb of Susan and The Syndicate was continuing to infuriate her. But she hadn't yet collected all the necessary resources to enact a plan that would simmer her down. For now, Susan would remain out of reach, but with a wry smile she thought, but *Trevor's not.*

"Veronica," she said, turning to face him and flashing a smile.

His smile widened, and he asked, "Can I buy you a drink?"

Pathetic, she thought. "No, thanks. I have one. But how about after this drink you and I get out of here?"

He tried to cover the shock at her forwardness, but she caught it. He cleared his throat and said, "Absolutely."

She picked up her martini glass and in one continuous drink emptied its contents. The olives were still affixed to the skewer now sitting in the empty glass. She removed it, laid the olives on her tongue, closed her lips, and slowly pulled back the empty skewer. Never removing her eyes from his, she slowly chewed, swallowed, and said, "I'm ready when you are."

Trevor led her from Hestia, taking the elevator down to the ground floor. He suggested the hotel next door, to which she replied, "How about your car?"

The look in his eyes said, "This girl's a freak." *If only he knew what was in store.*

His car, an Audi Q7 with third row seating, was parked on the fourth floor of the parking deck. He fumbled his keys from his pocket and finally managed to unlock the doors. She climbed into the backseat summoning him to join her and close the door.

He immediately dove in for a kiss, prodding his tongue into her mouth. She hadn't been touched by a man since before the death of her husband, and his forcefulness almost made her retch. But she was going to let this play out a little longer.

He groped her breast like a horny teenage boy with his left hand while he traced her spine at the small of her back with his right. A fleeting thought crossed her mind about him being a serial killer, and she smiled at the irony. *Best get this show on the road,* she thought, gingerly pulling away from him.

"What's wrong?" he asked, confusion etched on his face.

"Nothing really," she said sheepishly reaching into her purse. "You're breath's a little strong." She pulled out a bottle and handed it to him. "Here take this."

She could sense his skepticism rising, so she reached down to the hem of her shirt and lifted it over her head. Her lace bra brought his mind back into focus of what he desired, and without any further hesitation he sprayed twice.

His face winced from the taste. No doubt it tasted terrible. She quickly retrieved the bottle and leaned back away from him, watching with morbid fascination as he tried to speak but couldn't. He tried to clear his throat but couldn't. His eyes looked at her as if they were trying to speak for him, but alas they couldn't either.

The blood vessels in his eyes began to pulsate and grow larger as each breath grew shallower. He would've reached out to attack her if his arms, like everything else in his body, hadn't become paralyzed. Death was quick for Trevor, although for him it felt like an eternity.

She pulled her shirt back on, placed the bottle back in her purse, and stepped out of the vehicle. She then pulled her cellphone from her pocket and dialed the number labeled "Cleaners."

"This is Veronica. I have a job for you."

She relayed the details and disconnected the call. She momentarily considered her actions to be over the top for the evening but then quickly dismissed that notion. She looked out from the garage as dusk turned to darkness and thought, *I'll have to come for the sunset another day.*

13

On the north side of Charlotte, darkness began to descend on the city. The first hint of streetlights began to illuminate the road as artificial lights shone throughout homes across the city. In a gray Honda that blended with those of the neighborhood, the killer sat in deep thought. An issue and an opportunity had arisen that he hadn't expected. Now he needed to decide what to do about what he'd discovered.

The person who Detective Sampson and Special Agent Donatella had left the building with was a criminal profiler. And from what he'd been able to glean from his research, she was well renowned in her field. If what he read about the profiler was correct, she could lead them right to his doorstep, and he couldn't have this. Not before he had a chance to take down what would likely be his greatest conquest.

His target was both shrewd and careful, therefore ensnaring her would be a difficult if not impossible task. Thus, he took some time studying his prey. Her actions.

Her reactions. Her general state of being. And in his studies, he made a stark realization. The best way to get to her was through the peril of someone else.

Still, he was working at a disadvantage. At this point, he'd only heard and read of his prey's exploits. He hadn't had an opportunity to witness them firsthand. But as he sat outside the house of this criminal profiler, the person who was tasked with leading the FBI's hunt for him, a plan began to crystalize.

He'd already procured some hired hands to operate at his disposal, so it was now time to put them to work. In doing so, he could evaluate their skills in addition to those of his prey. He smiled, shifted the car into drive, and made a handsfree call that would set into motion a vital part of his masterplan.

HARMONY ELIZABETH BROWNING sat atop an oversized pillow situated on the floor, legs crossed, eyes closed. The calming melody of meditation music cascading the airways, the scent of lavender filling the room. She was on her third round of a well-practiced breathing ritual she'd honed over the years.

Meditation was a calming coping mechanism she undertook at an early age as a means to clear and focus her mind. Her childhood wasn't an uncommon one. She grew up as an only child, something experienced by forty-four percent of households, in a single-parent household after her parents' divorce, living with her dad until she went off for college. She was a daddy's girl through and through and didn't care who knew it. For so much of her life, he'd been the center of her universe. Even to this day, she called him every night to tell him she loved him.

She breathed air in through her nose, filling her lungs in the process, and slowly released it through her slightly parted lips with an extended ten count. The combination of breathing and counting helped abate the visions a childhood memory that periodically crept into her subconscious before she settled down to sleep.

An evening two weeks after her twelfth birthday, she was starting to watch a syndicated episode of *Criminal Minds*. Even at a young age, she had a curiosity to analyze behavior, patterns, and surroundings in a three-dimensional construct to determine a perpetrator. Conceptually, she understood the TV shows were scripted by writers, and thus things would inevitably be wrapped up with a pretty bow, but this wasn't always the case in real life.

Being an only child, friends were an important form of social engagement. And the previous year, her first in middle school, she felt a bit out of place. She and her dad had just moved to the area, so unlike the other newbies who had friends from elementary join them at the middle school, she was alone.

She watched as they told tales from their summer adventures, discussed their class schedules, and strategized about their after-school activities. Not having anyone to share her summer adventures with, she turned to her book while eating her lunch. As she read, she felt a presence looming over her. She looked up to find a girl she hadn't seen throughout the morning standing on the other side of the table.

"Whatcha reading there?" the girl asked with a small grin on her face.

Hesitantly she answered, "*Judy Moody Saves the World.*" She showed the cover to the book.

"Ah, yes. I remember that one. If memory serves me, it's book four in the series."

"Book three," she corrected.

"That's right," the girl giggled. "It is book three. They're all really good, at least in my opinion."

Feeling a little more at ease, she said, "Yes, this is my third time reading through the series."

The girl's smile widened as she outstretched her hand. "I'm Stacey."

"Harmony," she said in reply, shaking hands with the newcomer.

"Mind if I sit down?" Stacey asked eyeing the empty chair.

"No, not at all," came the immediate reply. This interaction was by far the longest she had all day, the only one she had all day. Not counting her saying "present" when the role was called.

Stacey slid the chair from under the table. Sitting down, she said, "Take it you're new to the school."

"New to the school and the state. My dad and I moved here over the summer from Ohio. I was shocked to learn I'd be starting middle school in the fall."

Her companion's eyebrows stitched together.

She continued, "In Ohio, elementary school goes through sixth grade. I was finally going to be at the top of the food chain at the school. Only to find out that middle school starts with sixth grade here in North Carolina. So back to the bottom I go."

The other girl smiled. "Well, it's not so bad here. I'm now in seventh grade, and I had a blast my first year. Looks like you're finished with your lunch. Why don't I give you the grand tour before break is over? I'll even introduce you to some of my other friends. I promise they aren't lame!"

"Count me in," Harmony responded, closing her book.

That conversation in the lunchroom was the beginning of an amazing friendship, one that came to a tragic end two weeks before the end of the school year.

Stacey and Harmony had gotten into a routine of meeting each other after school and walking home together. Each day, Stacey would be the first to their meeting spot around the corner from the school. They'd enthusiastically wave at one another and them begin their journey through the neighborhood.

The day was the same as others. The sun was shining, the air was warm, and the pollen had been washed away from the previous day's rainstorm. As Harmony turned the corner, their eyes connected, and they both broke out into a wave. Anticipating the pending conversation, she picked up speed.

In her memories, what happened next transpired in slow motion, but on that day, it took a matter of three seconds.

She could still hear the brakes screeching as the rubber from the tires burned on the concrete. The side panel of the van opened. A person, presumably male, fitted in all black, mask covering his face, jumped from the back. An arm snaked around Stacey, black glove covering her mouth while the other one yanked her from her feet. The figure leapt into the open door. An unseen person slammed it, while the driver left a second tread of rubber speeding off down the block.

Harmony didn't recall screaming but was assured days

later by the school's grief counselor that her screams brought the staff running. A search for her missing friend ensued, but the volunteers and the police were unable to locate the missing girl. However, two months after her abduction, thirty miles east of her home, Stacey's body was found unceremoniously dumped naked and bloodied on the side of the road.

Stacey had been the first in a series of similar abductions to plague the area, and in each case the local police department was unable to apprehend those responsible.

Browning had paid close attention to all the evidence the media shared with the public, wishing they could share more. It wasn't until the FBI became involved that a criminal profiler came onto the scene. The profiler properly identified the characteristics of the assailant, a substitute bus driver. With an arrest finally made in her friend's abduction, she felt closure that brought her some peace, but the visions continued in earnest.

What transpired all those years ago propelled her career trajectory. Browning inhaled deeply once again and slowly exhaled. The scent of lavender brought another hint of calm as she fought off the vision of Stacey's wide, pleading eyes above the outstretched glove over her mouth.

The subtle sounds permeating the room played in her mind as she opened her eyes. As with each night, she filed away that final vision, stood from her seated position, gathered up the pillow, and stowed it away in the closet. She turned down the volume of the music and picked up her phone.

After two rings, the call was answered. She said with glee in her voice, "Hi, Dad, how was your day?"

14

"Come on, Marcellous. Get a move on. Our guests will be here soon," Jasmyn yelled up the stairs. She walked over to Sebastian and began tugging at his shirt. "You know your daddy would lose his head if it wasn't connected to his shoulders." This elicited a squeal from the toddler. "No worries, you'll get your punctuality from your mama."

She licked her thumb and wiped a smudge from his cheek.

Marcellous appeared at the bottom of the stairwell. "You know, I heard that. And for the record, I'm nowhere near late. As long as I make an appearance before the first guest arrives, I'm doing well."

"Oh yeah. I'll remember that the next time you tell me I'm running late."

Marcellous shook his head. "Oh no. You aren't getting away with that one. Your late is us leaving the house five minutes after the event has started. In our sixty-two years of marriage, I don't recall us being on time to any event unless we are hosting."

She gave him a wry smile. "Sixty-two years, uh. Another item to tuck away for a rainy day. Besides, it's called being fashionably late. All eyes are on us when we make our grand entrance."

"Eyes in the forms of daggers," he said under his breath.

"What was that, dear?" she asked, raising an eyebrow.

He was preparing to mount a defense when the doorbell rang. "I think I better get that," he said, passing her a wink.

"Saved by the bell once again. Your luck will run out one of these days."

"But not today," he replied over his shoulder as he proceeded to the foyer with a bounce in his step. Looking through the windows that framed both sides of the door, he spotted Sal and Jane awaiting his arrival.

"Hey, guys," he said in greeting after opening the door. "Come on in." Jane leaned in, giving him a hug and a kiss on the cheek. Sal was the second through, shaking Marcellous's hand and handing him a bottle of chilled wine.

"I hope we aren't late," Sal said, patting Marcellous on the shoulder.

"Not at all. In fact, you're the first to arrive."

Jane shot Sal a look. "I told you we wouldn't be late. Rushing me again for no reason."

Marcellous smiled as he led them toward the family room. "Dinner's about done. You guys grab a seat, and I'll put this wine on ice. Can I pour either of you a glass?"

"I'll take one," Jane replied as she rushed over to swoop Sebastian into her arms.

"None for me," Sal said as he located a spot on the sofa and sat down. "I'll save mine for dinner."

"Dear, anything for you?" Marcellous asked Jasmyn as she hugged the Grandsons.

"Sure, I'll take a glass."

The doorbell rang once again. "I'll get it, hon. You finish up with the wine."

As she approached the front door, Jasmyn could hear the squeals of her son as a result of the tickle monster Jane had deployed. She opened the door to find Troy and Bethany standing on the other side.

"Hey, girl," Bethany cooed as the two ladies embraced. "I absolutely love your dress."

"This old thing? It's the first time I've worn it since giving birth to Sebastian."

"Well, you look gorgeous!"

"Thank you," Jasmyn said. "I'm still loving what you did with your hair. Blonde really suits you. Were you shocked when you saw it, Troy?"

"To say the least," he responded in a monotone voice.

"If it were up to Troy, I'd never change it."

"That's because you are already perfect," he said.

"Aww. Thanks babe," she said, leaning in to give him a kiss. "You sure do know how to make a girl smile."

Jasmyn motioned toward the family room. "The party's this way. Make yourselves at home. Marcellous is opening a bottle of wine if you're interested."

"I can go for a glass," Bethany said as they proceeded in the direction of the family room.

The ringing of the doorbell stopped Jasmyn in her tracks. "Looks like our final guests have arrived," she said, turning around and heading back to the door. She opened it to find Donatella and Sampson.

"I hope we aren't too late," Donatella said in her familiar southern drawl.

"Nope, you're right on time. Beth and Troy arrived, and the Grandsons were only here a few minutes ahead of them."

"We brought dessert," Sampson said, holding up a container. "My mom's famous pecan pie. Ten minutes in the oven at 350 degrees, and it'll be perfect. Picked up some vanilla ice cream as well."

"It's my favorite," Jasmyn said, smiling ear to ear. "Come, let's go to the family room where everyone else is gathered."

Upon reentry, Jasmyn noticed Jane and Beth fawning over Sebastian while Marcellous and Sal were in the kitchen deep in conversation. Troy was sitting, isolated, on the sofa seemingly preoccupied.

"Everyone's here. We have a few finishing touches before dinner is complete. In the meantime, mingle amongst yourselves. Donatella, Sampson, can I offer either one of you a glass of wine?"

"No, thank you," Donatella said.

"I'm good," replied Sampson. "Marcellous, we brought dessert. I've given Jasmyn the heating instructions."

"Excellent. Thank you," he responded, taking the pie and ice cream.

The visitors went into the family room while the Thompsons put the final touches on dinner. Jasmyn beamed as she watched their closest friends interacting and her son eating up all the attention. Heart full, she wrapped her arms around Marcellous's waist and gave him a hug from behind.

"What's that for?" he asked closing the oven and then turning to face her.

"I'm thankful for how everything turned out. I still think back to when I was kidnapped by that crazy woman at the direction of Terri Buckley. I was in danger. Our child was in danger. But through it all, I never gave up hope. Deep down, I knew you would find me. You're a good, no, you're a great husband, and I never want to take you for granted. Having everyone here today reminds me how close I was to never having this moment again. And damn it, I'm going to savor each one because you never know when it'll be the last one."

Marcellous and Jasmyn's eyes locked, and he said, "I'll never let anything happen to you or our family. Not to mention our son's godmother is a kick-ass FBI agent. She has a pure heart, and I know she'll always keep vigilant over our family as if it was her own. Heck, in some regards, we're the closest family she has."

Jasmyn wiped a tear from her eye. "You're right. But I sense an energy between her and Sampson I hadn't noticed before, one that may dispel your notion of us being her closest family."

They turned to face their guests, both observing the closeness the detective and the FBI woman shared while sitting in their living room. The timer disturbed their reverie, and Jasmyn announced, "Time to eat."

The three visiting couples drifted into the formal dining room to be greeted with an exquisite place setting and extraordinary center piece.

Jane was first to speak, "Jasmyn, you have outdone yourself. This table is to die for. And where on Earth did you find this centerpiece? It's gorgeous."

"Thanks, Jane. Beth and I picked up the components for the centerpiece, and I constructed it last night."

"Well, you have a hidden talent that is screaming to be let loose. You could surely start your own business."

Blushing, she said, "Thank you, but being a nurse is my calling. Who knows, once I retire, I may give it a go."

At the eight-person table, the Grandsons sat across from each other. Bethany and Troy sat next to Jane, while Donatella and Sampson sat next to Sal. The two seats at the head of the table were reserved for the evening's host and hostess with the highchair situated next to Jasmyn's chair.

Dinner proceeded as expected. Jasmyn started off the meal with a toast.

"I really wanted to bring all of you together this evening to tell you how grateful we are for your friendship. Being the newcomers in town and finding friends is hard, but faith brought us together, and circumstances cemented our bonds. Here's to our continued growth and everlasting friendship."

"I'll drink to that," Jane said as everyone began to clink their glasses together. With the toast out of the way, they started to eat. The meal from Chef Marcellous received raved reviews from the guests, with Sal and Sampson opting for seconds. The conversation flowed effortlessly, and Sebastian managed to keep all the food on his tray.

"Who's up for dessert?" Marcellous asked as he headed into the kitchen. A symphony of requests rang out from the group. "Coming right up," he added, making the final turn.

"So, Donatella, Sampson, what's the latest on your case involving the death of Detective Porter?" Sal inquired.

Sampson, who was still struggling with the death of his partner, said, "Her murder is still unsolved, but we have an angle we're following. We've been working with a colleague of Donatella's. She's provided some insight that may be useful."

"Such as..." Jane chimed in.

Donatella didn't want Sampson giving away too much, so she said, "Suffice it to say we are looking into all the murders conducted by this killer and searching for points of intersection."

"Interesting," Beth said. "I wouldn't think the detective and the other two victims crossed paths. The first two were closer in age. Hey, hon," she said, turning to Troy, who'd been quieter than normal. "The first victim was a student at your school. Did you ever meet her?"

All eyes shifted in the direction of Troy. He cleared his throat. "Yes, in fact she was a student of mine when she disappeared."

Beth eyed him for a minute. "You never told me that."

"There really isn't much to tell. The semester was almost over when she disappeared, and at the time there wasn't any hints of foul play. Her grades were not up to par, so I figured she simply dropped the class. It wasn't until later that this proved to be an incorrect assumption."

"How did she seem leading up to her disappearance?" Donatella asked.

"Nothing seemed out of the ordinary to me. With the number of students in my lecture, I hardly delved into the details of their lives."

"You're a creative writing professor, correct?" Sampson asked.

"That's correct."

"Anything show up in her writing that struck you as odd?"

Troy thought for a moment. "No, nothing I can think of. I wish I could me more help, but like I mentioned, I really didn't know her all that well."

"Hot pecan pie coming to a table near you," Marcellous said, entering the formal dining area carrying the evenings dessert.

"I've been waiting for this moment since the pie entered this house," Jasmyn said with her fork at the ready. This brought a laughter amongst the group that had momentarily grown tense with the conversation about Mandy Cox. With the smell of roasted pecans wafting through the air, the mood returned to normal, and a nice banter started up once again.

Twenty minutes after all desserts had been consumed the guest began to file out. Jane and Sal were the first to head for the exit, followed by Troy and Beth. Donatella was spending a few precious minutes with her godson while Sampson shared a few words with the Thompsons.

"Thank you again for inviting me and for being such great hosts. It makes me feel part of an extended family."

"Well," Jasmyn said a smile plastering her face, "I've only known Donatella a short period of time, but in that time I've never seen her light up around anyone like she does when you are around."

"Jasmyn," Marcellous said, elongating her name, "stop playing matchmaker. You must forgive her. She believes everyone should have someone and they should be with them right now. No time to waste."

Sampson laughed as Donatella approached. "It's all good. No harm here. I think she's wonderful."

"Who?" Donatella asked, holding Sebastian in her arms.

"Oh, no one. I think we should be headed out too so Marcellous and Jasmyn can get some rest and relaxation after a stellar dinner event."

Donatella raised an eyebrow as if she was going to challenge his statement. Instead, she said, "I think that's a good idea." She gave Sebastian a big squeeze and a kiss on the cheek. "You listen to your mom and dad." She handed him to Marcellous and leaned over to give Jasmyn a hug. "We'll see ourselves out. And again, thank you. I had a wonderful time."

"The pleasure is all mine," Jasmyn said as she pulled away from the embrace. "Are we still running in the morning?"

"Better believe it. I need to work off this pie I ate." They all erupted into laughter. Donatella and Sampson went through the foyer and out the door. Before they walked to the car, she turned to Sampson. "Did you observe what I observed while Troy was talking?"

"Yeah, I did. Deception. When asked about anything in her papers, he took some time to think. In doing so, he shifted his eyes top-right. I'm not sure what he's hiding, but he is hiding something."

"It may be nothing, but it's something we should look into."

Sampson thought back to a case the department worked before he became a detective. It turned out one of his closest friends had been killing women, and he was the one to break the case open.

He said, "It can be kind of weird looking into a friend."

Walking to the car, Donatella responded, "We aren't

15

Sal Grandson rolled out the bed at 5:45 a.m. on a Monday morning. Individual rays of sunshine were pressing through the window, illuminating the corner of the master suite. He found it increasingly hard to slide from the bed unnoticed because of the loose floorboards on his side. He found if he placed his foot closer to the edge of the board that the sound was muffled. But in the dark it was hard to gauge if he would land on the edge of the loose board or if the wrong step would cause Jane to stir.

Most days, he wouldn't give it a second thought. He'd hop from the bed, throw on his running clothes, and be out the house. But inevitably on his cheat meal day, the floorboard always managed to creek, which in turn would wake Jane. She'd wish him a good run and advise she'd have breakfast ready when he returned. Some days, he would forge forward and consume the doughnut he'd been salivating for all week. But often he'd sprint past the store and plan to make a stop the following week. But this morning he was resolute. The chocolate one covered with peanuts would be his, as long as he could leave the house without waking Jane.

He hoped the sunshine would provide some assistance with the darkness, but the timing was all wrong. He gingerly stepped down, wincing in anticipation of the sound. After a moment, he realized a sound hadn't been made. He smiled, figuring the worst was behind him and lifted himself from the bed. With his full weight now pressing down on the wooden floor, the floorboard groaned in protest. He shook his fist in the dark swearing under his breath.

Jane, who could sleep through a F5 tornado, was always awoken by the sound of the loose board. "Hey, Sal," she murmured, turning over to face him with her right eye partially open. "No run this morning?"

"No, not today. My mind has been working overtime since our dinner at the Thompsons. Last night after you went to bed, I did a little more digging into the background of Detective Porter. I called in a favor from my buddy Neil. Most times when I need something or someone found that doesn't want to be found, he finds a way to dig it up. The information is never free and typically comes with a favor to be curried in the future.

"He sent a response to my question in the middle of the night, and I couldn't help but read it. I'm still not sure if the information he provided will bear any fruit, but as a journalist I figured I should at least pull on the thread to see where it leads."

Jane opened her other eye and was now fully invested in what Sal was saying. "And what did the email say?"

"It appears Detective Elise Porter had two siblings, a

sister, Emma and a brother, Edward. He was the middle child, and then Emma came along later. It sounds like both Edward and Elise were extremely close. He ended up being confined to a mental institution, where he is to this day. The reason for his confinement wasn't made obvious in the details I received, but I'm hoping he could shed some light on his sister that we could use. I know it's a long shot, and it certainly couldn't hurt."

He began going to the door when he heard rustling of the sheets followed by Jane's feet hitting the ground. "I'm coming with you," she said as she turned on the light and headed to the bathroom.

"It's okay. I can handle this one. Besides, it could be nothing."

"Or it could be something. Plus, I don't have any other plans for the day. We can pay him a visit and then grab some breakfast. I heard there's a new vegan restaurant that opened, and I've been dying to try it out. Why don't you put on some coffee while I get ready? It won't take me long."

He groaned inwardly as the vision of the delectable doughnut vanished from his mind's eye. He simply replied, "Yes, dear."

Jane and Sal completed the two-hour journey to Triangle Springs Mental Institution and pulled into the parking area shortly after 8:40 a.m. During the drive, they contemplated how they would gain access to the younger Porter since they were not his kin.

Sal, who had broken into many secured buildings in his past, figured they could find the weakness in their security. From there they could get to his room. He'd already started mapping his plan until Jane pointed out that they didn't know Edward's room number. And even if they did, this place was likely locked down tighter than the places he'd broken into before.

Jane figured they could use a little social engineering to gain the access they needed. Wait until they found a group entering the facility and tag along. That would grant them entry into the building without being questioned. Sal was quick to point out that a group entering the facility was highly unlikely. It wasn't as if field trips were given. And then he piggybacked on Jane's original point, they didn't have a room number. He had to admit that he hadn't thought this one through, but he always found a way and was sure by the time they arrived that he'd have a plan.

Unfortunately, when they arrived a plan had yet to materialize, and they sat in the car spent on ideas. He rubbed his forehead between his thumb and index finger as he thought. It wasn't as if they were trying to land a man on the moon or cure cancer. He figured if he thought hard enough that a solution would present itself. But the harder he thought, the further away the solution seemed.

Thirty minutes after their arrival, he was preparing to give his brain a break, when a thought popped into his head. His sudden movement gave Jane a start, and she inquired, "What?"

"I have an idea, but it will require a white lie."

"I already told you that I'm not going to fake an illness so you can pretend you want to commit me as a patient. With my luck, they'll take me right away."

"No, it's not that, though I still think that's a viable backup plan. What if we claim to be neighbors of his sister Elise and tell them we were cleaning out her belongings and came across a letter addressed to Edward Porter with the institution's name on it. We can claim we drove it up here to give to him. This could be a way to solve our chief concern about not knowing which room he is in. Armed with that knowledge, we could pull from one of our other ideas to then gain access to Mr. Porter."

Jane pondered this for a moment and then said, "Didn't I suggest that earlier?"

"No, you suggested we pretend to be his kin. We decided that may not work, as we would likely need to be on the list to visit him. And lacking that, they may want to call someone to verify our claim."

"Hmm…if you say so, but I could have sworn I said this already. And considering I may have said it, this seems to be a good idea. I could write a letter and address it. Yep. Brilliant, if I do say so myself."

Sal refrained from any additional challenges as he watched Jane pull some paper from her bag. He was willing to bet she had an envelope in there as well.

"What should it say?" she asked clicking the end of her pen.

"I don't think it matters," Sal replied. "I doubt they plan to read it to him, and once he gets it –"

"Yeah, when he gets a letter from his murdered sister, it better say something profound or he will be devastated."

He hadn't considered this, as his only thought was trying to get into the room with Edward. But she had a point. "Why don't you make it a farewell letter? One that would be sent to him in the event she was killed in the line of duty. Tell him how much she loved him. How she wished she could spend more time with him. Tell him that he was never far from her heart and that she thought about him every day. Tell him that even though she was now gone, they would be together again."

"Sal, you old teddy bear. That's perfect," she said as she began to scribble onto the paper. She spent fifteen minutes crafting the letter before giving it a final read. She dug back into her bag and retrieved a package containing 3x5 brown envelops. She took her time expertly folding the letter and sliding it into place. Sal's amazed expression elicited a response. "I've done this a few times," she said sealing the letter.

"You don't say," he responded, shaking his head. "Is there anything you can't do?"

"Stick around long enough, and you may uncover a flaw or two. Now, are you ready to get this show on the road?"

"As ready as I'll ever be."

They proceeded to the entrance and along the way decided Jane would do the talking while Sal would keep a keen eye for any useful data. Upon entering the facility, they were surprised at the quietness. They were immediately greeted by the receptionist at the front desk.

"Good morning, and welcome to Triangle Springs. What brings you in today?"

"My name is Penelope Betts, and I hope you'll be able to point me in the right direction. My neighbor recently passed away, and upon cleaning out her belongings we came across a envelop that I believe may belong to a patient in your care."

"Oh dear. I'm sorry to hear about your neighbor. I'd be happy to assist."

"Thank you." She reached into her bag and retrieved the letter. She read from the envelop, "Edward Porter. Triangle Springs. That's all it says," she said, handing the letter to the woman. As she did, she noticed the expression of the woman darken.

"Ms. Betts," she said cautiously, "I'm afraid I have some bad news for you. We had a patient here by the name of Edward Porter, but unfortunately he's no longer with us."

"I see. Are you at liberty to inform us where he's been transported to? We'd really like to pass along this letter from his sister. It seems she really wanted him to have it."

"I'm sorry, I think you misunderstood me." She looked around and lowered her voice. "Mr. Porter isn't with us any longer because on Friday night he took his own life."

Jane involuntarily shot a hand to her mouth. A moment of dread and sorrow overtook her, and Sal stepped in, "That is terrible, and we are so sorry to hear that."

"It was totally unexpected, but we suspect the loss of his sister drove him to such drastic measures. Edward was well liked by the staff. He was pleasant to be around and never gave us any trouble. Many staff members, me included, were crushed by his death."

"Understandable," Sal said. "It sounds like he left an impression on the staff, on you. I'm sorry for your loss."

"Thank you," she said, holding back tears. "I'm sorry you came all this way for nothing. If you'd only come a day earlier, we could have included the letter with his other belongings that were mailed to his sister."

Jane regained her composure, "By chance do you still have the address for the sister. Maybe we can send the letter to her. It feels wrong for us to throw it away."

"Sure. Let me grab that for you." She pressed a few keys on the keyboard. Scanned the screen, maneuvered the mouse, and clicked it a few times. The sound of the printer transferring data to paper filled the room. Once done, the receptionist retrieved the paper and handed it to Jane.

"Here you go. I pray that family finds peace. Losing two

family members in quick succession is enough to drive you mad."

Sal and Jane thanked her for the assistance and walked back to the car. Inside, Jane said, "How awful. That poor boy. I'm sure the family is heartbroken." She turned to him with fierce determination in her eyes. "We can't allow his death, and for that matter her death, to be in vain."

"What do you have in mind?" Sal asked.

"Let's go talk with the sister to see if she can shed any light on this situation. And even if she can't, we should at minimum offer our condolences and then do everything we can to unearth any details that could lead Donatella and Sampson to this monster."

Sal reached over and took the paper from her hand. He entered the address and said, "Then let's do this."

16

The Monday-morning-rush-hour traffic on the interstate was something H.E. Browning had trouble rationalizing. When the roads were properly engineered and when drivers obeyed the traffic laws, this type of standstill should never happen. There were drivers in a rush to get nowhere fast or people completing their morning grooming because they couldn't find the time to address this as part of their daily at-home routine. And this morning, she found herself sandwiched between a large green dump truck on her left and an eighteen-wheeler on her right.

Furthermore, there always seemed to be a bottleneck at the same location every day regardless of the hour, and today she was smack dab in the middle of it. This diverted her mind to the point regarding poor engineering. Not to mention the weatherman was calling for thunderstorms scheduled to appear sometime between early and mid-morning. *Such an imprecise science,* she thought. But since these were issues she couldn't resolve, she used this quandary to map out her morning.

With the profile requested by SA Dabria now complete, she could move on to the connection regarding the murder of three gangbangers in the projects and a white-collar worker in Ballantyne. She'd been following the news coverage outlining the gruesome way the three victims had been eliminated. While officials were stopping short of saying the two crimes were connected, she found it highly plausible. To date, no departmental request had been made, but she found looking through such cases kept her mind sharp.

As the mosaic of brake lights in front of her was beginning to dissipate and the rumble of thunder cascaded a few miles away, she looked ahead to see mile marker six. *Right on schedule*. This was always the clearing point when heading north on Interstate-77. Her thoughts returned to what she needed to accomplish before noon. *I owe a response to UNCC*, she thought adding it to her mental to do list.

They were searching for a guest to speak with their Criminology 221 class. It would be for the next semester, but they wanted a commitment as part of the draw for class registration. She'd agreed to give them an answer by Wednesday's deadline and saw no need in putting it off any longer. The commitment was minimal, four talks spread over the course of two weeks. *And I'd have plenty of time to prepare.* She already knew she would honor the request, and it was now time to make it official.

Browning was mentally moving on to the next item on her list when she heard the dump truck rev its engine followed by that of the eighteen-wheeler. She thought this odd, as the traffic hadn't cleared enough for them to make any significant movement. They were going about thirty-five mph, well under the posted speed limit, with no room to maneuver considering there were only three lanes.

The eighteen-wheeler was the first to act, barreling into the back of the much smaller sedan in front of it. The sound of metal against metal filled the air as the smaller vehicle was catapulted forward, causing it to lose control and veer off into the berm. The semi continued to accelerate, hitting the F-150 now standing in its way. The unsuspecting driver of the vehicle attempted to speed up, but with the larger vehicle already accelerated, it too was pushed forward, slamming into the car in front of them.

Meanwhile, the dump truck to her left was dispatching of cars in its wake, accelerating with the effort. Unsure what to do, Browning began to decrease her speed while simultaneously activating her car's handsfree calling feature.

"Call home office" she said calmly as the scene played out in front of her. After two rings, the call was answered. She said, "This is Agent Browning. There is a semi-truck and a dump truck running cars off the road. Traveling northbound 77, mile marker seven. Call EMS and the police. They –"

She stopped as the dump truck veered into her lane, decreasing its speed as well. The back hatch dropped to the ground, and sparks began to fly as it slid across the concrete. She could see the brake lights on both sides of the truck illuminate, causing Browning to slam on her brakes.

From the back of the truck, three masked men began opening fire while two more leapt to the ground. She ducked as the rounds flew. She could hear glass shattering and projectiles tearing through aluminum.

"The dump truck has stopped, and three men have emerged from the back. They've started opening fire," she yelled into the phone. "We're all trapped. Send help now!"

It hadn't donned on her in that frantic moment that her vehicle had not been targeted by the gunfire. Instead, she heard her passenger side window being smashed, glass cascading down over her. A hand reached in, unlocked her door from the inside, and yanked it open. Two strong hands seized her by her arms and dragged her from the car. She screamed louder than she ever had in her life, but it was drowned out from the cacophony of gunshots erupting around her. She tried to kick, but her legs were grabbed by the second man.

The sound of bullets firing stopped and was replaced by screams from those who had been around and behind her vehicle, along with the intensity of thunder booming nearby. Tucked away in the emergency lane were two black Suburbans with tinted windows. The men who were firing from the dump truck hopped into the first one. The backdoor of the second one was pushed open from the inside. The two men carrying Browning tossed her through the opening and slammed the door shut.

Browning bounced once prior to settling on the bench seat. Before she could discern her surroundings, she felt a sting press against her neck. Two more doors opened elsewhere in the vehicle and were immediately slammed shut. The last thing she heard before she blacked out was rain splattering on the vehicle's roof and a voice saying, "We got her."

DONATELLA HAD BEEN in Brent's Coffee Shop when she received a priority notification from FBI communications. It was labeled "Potential Agent Abduction." Although it was considered serious, she rarely put much stake in them. With the entire department looking for the missing agent, they were typically recovered soon thereafter. And in almost every single instance, it was an agent undercover who lost communication with his or her handler.

Curiosity got the better of her, and she opened the notification to see which agent was missing. Upon reading the name H.E. Browning, she bolted from her chair and sprinted toward the door. Her quick and sudden movements garnered stares and murmurs from the patrons as she dashed out the door. She hurried to her car as the rain that had been threatening all morning had begun to rear its head.

Browning was an office agent, not a field agent, so for her to be missing generated immediate red flags. Donatella didn't believe in coincidences, and for her to go missing shortly after providing a profile could only mean one thing. The killer could feel the noose tightening and, worse, knew Browning was providing the clues that could bring him down.

Once in her car, she finished skimming the notification. Her last known whereabouts was on 77 northbound between mile markers seven and nine. Donatella was slightly north of this location, and from what she read this would be the best direction for her approach. She sped toward the scene, tires finding new traction with the wet road. She was hoping for the best but mentally preparing for the worst.

When she arrived, police, EMS, and the fire department were on the scene.

Three police officers were cordoning the area, which looked like a war scene. Other officers were questioning those who had not been injured in the attack.

The EMS personnel was moving at a frenetic pace. They were dividing into two parties. Those triaging the victims with non-life-threatening injuries on the scene. While the second group was transporting victims with critical injuries to the awaiting ambulances.

The fire department was there to suppress any fires, but since there appeared to be minimal threat of that, they aided the EMS team.

Donatella approached the officer standing post. They made eye contact, and as she drew near, he said in a soft but firm voice, "Sorry, ma'am, this area is off limits."

Donatella showed her credentials. "Special Agent Dabria. Who's in charge?"

He eyed her badge and said, "Officer Hand was first on scene. He's leading the questioning of the witnesses." He pointed southeast of their direction.

She headed that way, observing the resulting chaos. Shattered glass strewn about, bullet riddled vehicles, and varying blood puddles being washed away in the rain.

She found the man she assumed to be Officer Hand, a squat, balding man with ample girth. Full salt and pepper beard with a baritone voice.

"Here's my card," he said to the witness. "If you can think of anything further, please give me a call."

He turned to find himself face-to-face with Donatella. She said, "Officer Hand, I presume. I'm Special Agent Donatella Dabria."

"What interest does the FBI have in this case?"

"One of our agents called in the incident as it took place in real-time. She has since gone missing. I'm trying to find out what happened to her."

"Sorry to hear about your colleague. Details are a bit sketchy, but I'll share what I've gathered thus far."

Before he could get started, another figure emerged from behind Donatella.

"Officer Hand, Donatella," a familiar voice said.

She turned. "Detective Sampson, what are you doing here?"

"I heard what happened and came over to see if I could lend a hand."

She found this odd considering he was on leave, so she was curious how the news made it to his ears.

"Officer Hand was about to give some insight on what he's been able to ascertain."

"Will you be taking over the case?" the officer asked.

"No, I'm here strictly on an informational basis. A detective will be assigned."

Hand gave him a quizzical look but proceeded, "Witnesses say a semi and a dump truck pulled forward from the slow and fast lanes. The semi accelerated through the slow lane, sending cars off the highway. Then they noticed the dump truck maneuvering into the middle lane, the back opened, and bullets started flying. One witness said the men advanced in the direction of the car directly behind the truck and grabbed the driver. She couldn't tell if the driver was male or female. They then walked to SUVs on the side of the highway and then drove off."

"That must have been Browning," Donatella said and started walking in the direction of the dump truck.

"Thank you," Sampson offered as he turned to follow the agent.

He caught up with her at the car directly behind the dump truck.

"Notice anything strange about this vehicle?" she asked when he arrived.

He looked it over and said, "Nothing out of the ordinary."

"That's exactly it. Every other car is riddled with bullet holes, but the only thing wrong with Browning's vehicle is the busted window, which means –"

"She was the target all along," Sampson finished. "But why would someone target her?"

Before she could answer, Sampson's cellphone vibrated in his pocket. "Hold that thought," he said so he could answer the phone.

"This is Sampson."

"Detective Carl Sampson, Charlotte Metro Police Department," the modulated voice said. Sampson immediately grabbed Donatella's attention and placed the phone on speaker.

"Looks like you've garnered some assistance to find me. What happened to it being 'let the best man win?' Seems you are going a long way to tilt the playing field in your favor. Since you called in some reinforcements, I did too. And right now, my reinforcement has that nosey FBI profiler. But I'll give you a chance to redeem yourself. Let's see if you can save her, unlike what you were able to do with your partner, Elise Porter.

"This time, I'm not going to waste time with any hints. I'm going to simply tell you where she is being held. She's at Carowinds Amusement Park, and I suggest you hurry, because time is of the essence and things could get very hairy for the agent."

"If any harm comes her way, there isn't a corner of this Earth you'll be able to hide," Donatella said.

"Special Agent Dabria, good to make your acquaintance. No need for the melodramatics. Our paths will cross soon enough. Until then, I suggest you get moving. The clock is ticking."

The call disconnected. Sampson said to Donatella, "You know this is a trap."

"Indeed, it is. Now it's time we go rescue Agent Browning and dispose of anyone who stands in the way."

17

Donatella crossed over the North Carolina state line into South Carolina, dropping her speed from the 100 mph she'd been traveling so she could better navigate the exit on the slick road. Upon leaving I-77 south, she headed west on Carowinds Blvd with Sampson following closely behind.

They blew past the parking attendant's gate, accelerating through the empty parking lot in search of the entrance. This unscheduled visit to the park would be the first time Donatella had been on the grounds, thus putting her at a severe disadvantage. Not only was she blind to her adversary and their exact motive, but she was also blind to the operating theater.

She skidded to a stop near what she figured was the entrance, while recalling that the park had been in the news recently. The closure of the amusement park headlined the news cycles for the better part of a week. Their marquee roller coaster, Demon's Breath, which locals dubbed "The Demon," had been shut down because of a second malfunction. With this being the main attraction that drew crowds from around the US, the park had been shut down until further notice.

Demon's Breath, at 433 ft tall, was the second tallest roller coaster in the United States behind Kingda Ka at Six Flags Great Adventure located in Jackson, New Jersey. It reached a top speed of 115 miles per hour during its 433 ft drop and included its trademarked 360 degree twisting loop on the ascent after the drop.

And yet as Donatella and Sampson approached the entrance, The Demon was running through its paces on the tracks in the middle of the amusement park.

"How do you want to handle this?" Sampson asked, slamming a magazine into his Glock 43x.

Visibility was becoming problematic, as the rain was now coming down in sheets. Donatella retrieved her jacket and utility belt from her trunk. She slid the jacket on and fastened the utility belt around her waist. She fingered the five-digit code into her gun safe and retrieved her SIG Sauer P226.

She slipped it into her holster and said, "It's clear they aren't averse to violence, so protect yourself. And with the park being closed to the public, anyone moving around is likely a combatant. Engage with extreme prejudice."

They proceeded toward the entrance, setting off the metal detectors as they passed through. Aside from the running of the roller coaster, the immense amusement park was eerily silent.

Donatella could sense the fine hairs on the back of her neck beginning to prickle as her mind continued to remind her to be diligent. Although it was quiet and appeared to be vacant, her senses could detect pending danger. She looked in the direction of Sampson, and from the way his eyes were darting back and forth while he processed what his eyes were seeing, he too was on high alert and ready to act.

As partners go, his actions at the Cleveland Museum of Art had already proved to her that he could be trusted and that he could handle himself well in a gunfight. This materialized into a comfort she had never experienced, and for once it was refreshing.

"They're drawing us to the tracks," Sampson said, heading in its direction. "My guess is we will find Browning in the vicinity in addition to the welcoming party. You ready?"

She was prepared to answer when she noticed an ominous red glow ahead. Her mind filtered out the question and instead focused on the source of the light. The number 26 was being shown from a digital display near where The Demon started and subsequently came to an end. The sound of the cars making their approach drew her attention. She turned to look, and there she noticed the body of Agent Browning tied to the seat. It barreled past the start, and an audible tick was heard from the direction of the digital display. She drew attention back in that direction and noticed it now read 25.

A crude wiring system was present and running in numerous directions from the display. She allowed her eyes to follow one strand to find C4 attached to the structure. Her eyes darted back to the display and followed another strand, which led to another bundle of C4. At the speed the Demon's Breath was traveling, if the C4 didn't bring down the entire structure, the cars would catapult through the air with only a crash against the ground stopping its momentum.

"C4 attached to the track," she said.

"Yeah, I noticed," Sampson responded. "And to make matters worse, it looks like someone has destroyed the controls. There's no way to stop it from here."

The coaster came speeding by again, bringing with it a gust of stale wind.

Donatella reached into her pocket and pulled out a square plastic case about three inches long. She opened it and plucked an earpiece from within. "Place this into your ear. It works on a private frequency that will allow us to keep in constant contact. We will need to split up. See if you can locate the main switch that's operating Demon's Breath and shut it down. The ride takes roughly thirty seconds to complete, and the counter is already down to twenty-four. Which means we only have twelve minutes before detonation."

Sampson took the earpiece and placed it into his ear. "You know this is what they want, to separate us."

"Indeed, I do," she said in her calm, honeyed voice. "And that was a mistake."

She continued in the direction of the ride while Sampson took off in search of the control room. She watched as the coaster was bending the last curve and heading back in the direction of the starting location. The countdown ticked, 23, she thought as she focused in on her mission.

Her senses screamed, *danger,* and without a hesitation she dropped to the ground. The falling rain patterns were displaced, and she could feel a gust of wind flow overhead and from behind. She spun and through the driving rain could see the outline of a man slightly off balance wielding a cylindrical object. He pivoted and with determined aggression lifted the object and brought it down with all his might. Donatella managed to dodge to the left, barely escaping the blow as the object connected with the ground. Even in this rain, if it was metal, she would have heard it clang against the concrete. However, from the muted thud she determined his weapon of choice was likely a wooden bat.

Again, her attacker was on the prowl and used his momentum to spin 360 degrees while moving to his right. He spun into a backhand attack that this time connected with the agent. The force of the blow knocked Donatella from her feet and sent her careening across the slick surface.

The impacts from the bat and the ground knocked the air from her lungs, as she gasped trying to suck in some air. Eyes closed and searching for oxygen, she could sense he was closing in and preparing to strike again. She rolled to her right to create distance from another blow and to find time to rise to a standing position. This move brought her in direct contact with a second attacker she had yet to notice.

Pain shot from her ribs to her brain as her body registered the kick she received to her midsection. She chided herself for assuming there was only one, a mistake she would not make again. In that moment, as the pain flowed through her body, her Krav Maga training flashed and focused her mind.

An unfamiliar battleground. An undetermined number of enemies. A countdown ticking in the background. She slowed her breathing, cleared her mind, and sensed her surroundings. The rain was a constant that she filtered and drew on the subtle changes in the environment.

A heavy step that splashed in a puddle with the telltale signs hitting her face horizontally, not vertically. The assailant was preparing to stomp down on her face. Her hand, which had already been near her side from the natural response of being kicked in that area, extracted a throwing knife. In one fluid motion, she brought the knife to her face and with both hands pointed the tip up.

The downward power of the stomp mixed with her upward thrust of the knife forced the blade through the heel of the shoe and into the skin. She didn't wait for the impending body to hit the ground. She simply moved on to the next objective, getting to her feet.

She ignored the pain, as she'd encountered worse, and deftly sprung to her feet, eyes open and searching out the next threat. It didn't take long as the man wielding the bat was winding up to swing again. Though powerful when the bat struck, his execution was slow.

Donatella planted her feet firmly into the ground. With the power in her base and force from her speed, she jabbed him in the solar plexus with the palm of her right hand. His body bowed like a boomerang and the bat dropped from his grasp. Instinctively, she caught the bat by the barrel with her left hand, brought it across her body, and backhanded him in the face with the handle. There was an audible crack, presumably his jaw, as he crumbled to the ground.

She spun, peering through the rain for additional threats, but none were present. *At least not for now,* she thought. The countdown timer read 21 as she pressed forward.

THREE YEARS AGO, when Sampson was still on the beat, he along with several other officers from his department had taken a tour at Carowinds. While domiciled in South Carolina, since the park straddled the state line, they were briefed on the security measures. Strictly a precautionary measure should an attack transpire on the grounds, the owners and the mayor wanted to ensure the public could be kept safe.

Precautionary measure my ass, Sampson thought as he trudged through the pouring rain. As he navigated the final bend that led to the control center, his peripheral vision picked up movement off to his right. The words from Donatella replayed in his mind, "And with the park being closed to the public, anyone moving around is likely a combatant. Engage with extreme prejudice."

He turned right to determine if there was a potential threat, but his mind was slow to register the figure charging from his left. The slick concrete felt frictionless as they slid across the ground. The figure on top of him had Sampson outweighed and out-leveraged. Once their momentum stopped the figure began to pummel Sampson. A one-two blow to the left rib followed by the right stung, but Sampson spent countless hours sparring at the precinct, so the impact was minimal.

Before his attacker could strike again, Sampson reached up, grabbed his shirt, and with his legs and arms working in unison jerked his body to the left. The man landed on the ground with a silent thud, water splashing all around him. The man's girth betrayed his quickness, as he was to his feet a fraction of a second prior to Sampson. He began to charge again, but this time Sampson was prepared and side stepped the attempt.

The countdown clock was only present near the coaster and was out of his view. This heightened his sense of urgency to dispose of this foe as quickly as possible, because he didn't have a clue regarding how much time was remaining. Playing defense would draw out the conflict longer than necessary, so Sampson shifted immediately into offense.

He stalked in the direction of his assailant, who was taken aback by the move. He began to settle into a fighting stance, but Sampson darted in his direction with a headbutt to the face. A stream of blood poured from his target's nose. Sampson grabbed him by the shoulders and yanked his torso down. He brought his knee up to meet his assailants face, finishing the nose break that the headbutt started.

The attacker dropped to a knee, and Sampson finished him off with a chop to the back of the neck. The assailant crumpled to the ground, face down in a puddle of rainwater. Sampson took a moment to compose himself, and prior to continuing his journey to the control room, he pulled the unconscious man away from the puddle and turned him on his side. Unsure how long he'd be unconscious, Sampson affixed a pair of flex cuffs to his ankles and wrist. He reminded himself there was a more pressing concern and pushed ahead.

The door for the control room had been kicked in and haphazardly closed, barely hanging on the hinges. He strained, listening at the door focusing through the rain, but couldn't hear any sound coming from inside. He cautiously opened the door, hand hovering over his weapon. He soon realized no one was inside and sped to the master controls.

A chorus of thunder serenaded in the background as Sampson looked at them. It took a moment before he found the one he was looking for. He prepared to turn it off when he spotted a cord running from the box that appeared out of place. He followed it to the underside of the table and immediately paused.

Affixed to the bottom side of the table was a brick of C4 with a receiver protruding from it. The gravity of the situation became apparent. He stood from his stooped position and radioed Donatella.

As Donatella continued in the direction of Demon's Breath, a thought was beginning to surface. But before it could become fully formed, Samson was calling in on the comms.

"I'm at the control room, but I think we have a problem."

"What is it?" she yelled over the pouring rain.

"The controls for the coaster have been rigged with C4. I could try to disarm it, but I'm out of practice, and I'm afraid we will run out of time. Also, it has a receiver of some sort attached to it, which means somewhere on this park is the key for disarming this bomb and likely the ones on the track. My guess is it's situated somewhere high to reduce any possible interference."

Donatella began looking around.

He paused for a moment and continued, "I'm sure this goes without saying, but there are limited possible outcomes –"

She chimed in, "Yeah. If I don't find the transmitter,

either the countdown on the ride will reach zero. That would spell certain doom for Browning. Or..."

Sampson picked up the thread, "Or I flip the switch, stopping the car and saving Browning, but at the same time detonating the C4 in here."

The thought that tried to surface before the call came fighting back to the forefront. Something about this entire scene felt wrong somehow. In a park of this size, there would be an infinite number of locations to stash the transmitter so that it would never be found. The answer became crystal clear.

Donatella looked up while squinting through the rain. *There you are*, she thought. "I've gotta go," she said, ending the transmission and running to the base of The Demon.

She arrived at the back side of the ride where she found the maintenance entrance unlocked and the door wide open. *An invitation. I guess I shouldn't keep them waiting.* She idly noted the condition of the ride, noting it probably needed to be inspected soon.

She climbed the stairs two steps at a time, feverishly ascending to the top. The rain made the steps slick, but they also provided a modicum of cover from the elements. She continued to grow weary of the day's events, but she stayed vigilant and knew better than taking anything for granted. Underneath the massive structure, she no longer had visibility on the timer. But she calculated she had five minutes remaining or ten more loops along the tracks. At her current speed, it would take her another minute to reach her destination, so she increased to three steps at a time to cover additional distance at the same speed.

Within forty seconds, she'd come level with the transmitter that sat equal distance from her current position and the far end on the other side. There were numerous footholds above and below where the object sat with varying assurances of stability. She took a few breaths to map out her route as the ride completed another loop, leaving her with less than three minutes to accomplish this task.

A direct route proved troublesome, as some of the footholds appeared weathered, but she mapped out a plan and set off. In her current elevated position, the wind gust and the intensity of the rain had both increased. Her first three steps went according to plan, but as she drew closer to the middle, the structure seemed to sway as another gust arrived. She tightened her grip and paused, giving the wind a chance to die down. She continued meticulously navigating toward the center when she heard two popping sounds over the howl of the wind and the pounding of the rain. She discounted it as Sampson firing his weapon at someone or someone firing at him, though it didn't sound like gunshots.

She pressed forward when two additional pops, like the first, seemed to echo across the park. As Donatella began shifting her weight from her trail foot to her lead foot, the platform she was stepping on was slicker than the others. At the same time, the railing that she'd been gripping for support had been the source of the popping sounds. It immediately began to pull away from the structure just as Donatella grabbed it to steady herself from slipping on the platform. Simultaneously, another gust of wind pushed the special agent off balance.

The handrail lost two more bolts as the wind, her weight, and the growing momentum carried the handrail and the agent away from the structure. She began running scenarios through her mind as the vibration of the running coaster was causing havoc on her grip. Meanwhile the countdown timer ticked off an additional digit. From her current position, she could read the numbers on the clock now at 3. *A minute and a half*, she thought as another bolt, maybe two, gave way.

In her suspended animation, she had limited options and little time. She spoke calmly into her earpiece communication, "Carl, are you still in the control room?"

"I am."

"In thirty seconds, pull the switch and stop the ride."

He hesitated and then said, "But the C4."

"Thirty seconds." She grabbed the railing tighter with her left hand, reached down to her right ear, and removed the communication earpiece, allowing it to drop to the ground below.

She reached down to her utility belt, unlatched her gun, and in a practiced motion pulled it from the holster while flipping the safety. She raised her weapon, took aim, and fired two shots in quick succession. Both missed to the right. The rain-slick handrail was beginning to impact her grip. She pushed that to the back of her mind as she corrected her aim and slowed her breathing. As she squeezed the trigger, two more bolts popped in sequence, causing the railing to drop a few inches and the bullet to miss wildly. This drop caused her body to jolt, the handrail to bow, and her pointer finger and thumb to lose connection with the railing.

The thirty-second timeline she'd given Sampson was ticking in her mind. If she didn't get this right, he'd blow himself up all because she told him to. Her rotator cuff was starting to stiffen as her body weight and gravity were pulling her toward the ground. She raised her gun once again, and without overthinking the shot, she fired off five.

She was rewarded with the transmitter bursting into pieces, shredding apart as each bullet found its mark. However, her triumph was short lived. The recoil sent additional vibrations through her body, causing her to lose the remaining grip she had on the handrail.

18

Donatella rotated head over feet as the laws of physics propelled her toward the ground. She replayed the shots in her mind, and the sparks from the transmitter told her that Sampson would be safe, and in turn so would Agent Browning. The rain pelted her free-falling body, leaving her helpless to whatever would happen next.

The dark cloud cover in the sky and the dark asphalt below made it hard to distinguish between the two. She closed her eyes as the vision of her mom and her dad took form. In this moment of reflection, she realized she'd spent more time without them than she had with them. She often wondered what a reunion with them would feel like and often digressed wondering if she would feel anything when she was gone. Feelings or not, their reunion would be long overdue.

Her mind slowed everything down as her body hurled for its date with the waiting arms of the ground. Her parents were holding hands, and she caught the hint of a smile from her dad prior to locking eyes with her mom. In her mom's hazelnut eyes, she saw herself, a reflection of the woman she had grown to be. The FBI agent. The protector of the innocent. The godmother to Bree and Sebastian. The friend to the Thompsons, Grandsons, and Evans. The – she wasn't sure how to categorize her relationship with Sampson.

The blinked, and the focus shifted from her mother's eyes to her ageless, beautiful face. Her mother smiled like her father as Donatella realized the reflection of herself was how her parents saw her in that moment. Her mom mouthed two words that reverberated loudly in her psyche, "Not now."

Her parents faded away into the background, and Donatella felt a series of micro explosions detonate around her body. The pouring rain suddenly stopped as her body leveled out from the constant spinning. She opened her eyes to realized she was engulfed in a protective bubble seconds before she collided with the ground. The impact caused her to bounce several times before coming to a complete stop.

She looked in the direction of Demon's Breath to find it sitting still at the starting gate. She also noted the countdown timer at come to rest at 2. She laid her head back, realizing the danger had come to an end.

It wasn't long before Sampson was at her side using a utility knife to puncture the protective cover. It took several attempts, but he managed to create a hole big enough to communicate with the agent.

"Are you okay? What in the hell is this thing?"

"It's a long story," she said as the phone in her pocket

began to vibrate. She fished the phone to realize it was BJ calling in.

She tapped the green phone icon and placed the phone to her ear. She couldn't get a word out before BJ launched in.

"Agent Dabria, I received notification that your protection deployed near Carowinds Amusement Park. What's going on there?"

"A long story," she said. "Better question is how you knew the protection deployed."

"Oh, didn't I mention that? In the case of a fall that activates the suit, a beacon is sent to me with your location."

"We really need to have a talk about boundaries," she said as Sampson continued prodding at the bubble. "And thank you. It worked exactly as you stated it would."

"Never a doubt in my mind," he boasted.

"Now," she said, trying to sit up, "how do I get out of this thing?"

"There should be a blue button directly above your head." She looked up, noticing the button for the first time. "Press that for three seconds to make the protective bubble deflate.

She advised Sampson to step back. Unsurprisingly, the bubble deflated, and she was again greeted by the rain. Sampson reached down to help her up, and when she was standing erect, he pulled her in for a hug.

"I'm happy you're okay," he said as sirens could be heard approaching in the distance.

She returned the gesture before she shifted back into business. "We need to check on Browning," she said, taking off in that direction.

When they arrived, they found her tied to the safety bar, mouth gagged and drenched from the relentless rain.

Sampson used his knife to sever the binds while Donatella removed the gag. Once freed, Sampson helped her from the car. She stood on unsteady legs as Sampson helped her over to a bench that was used to house the belongings of those preparing to ride.

"Thank you," she said in Sampson's direction. "Thank you both. If it wasn't for you –"

"If it wasn't for us, you wouldn't have been in this situation," Donatella said.

"You have no control over that," Browning offered. "All I know is you both did everything possible to ensure I can see another day. And for that I'm eternally grateful."

"You're welcome," Sampson said.

They could hear rustling from below and a male voice. "Paramedics. Is anyone up there?"

"Yes," Donatella answered. "We have one person who needs to be transported to the hospital and evaluated."

"I don't –" Browning began saying before Donatella cut her off.

"You have a nasty gash, and it's better to play it safe. Furthermore, I'm going to call the agency and have agents posted at your room."

Two medics arrived, gurney in tow. Browning was still shaky on her feet, so they placed her on the gurney and wheeled her out.

By the time Sampson and Donatella reached the ground level, they spotted police officers rounding up the men Donatella had her confrontation with. She stopped and turned to Sampson. "Did anything strike you as odd about this encounter?"

He shot her a quizzical glare as he thought. After a moment he said, "No, is there something I'm missing?"

"The people responsible for abducting Browning shot up a major highway to grab her, presumably working at the behest of the person we are pursuing."

"Okay."

"And yet, the two men I fought weren't carrying any guns." She could see him replaying the confrontation he had.

"You're right. The person I tangoed with wasn't packing either."

She continued, "I also had this feeling that I was being watched."

Sampson said, "You're right. I witnessed movement coming from two different directions before my quarry started, but I only fought with one man."

"It finally donned on me that they were not trying to kill us. They were there simply to fight us."

"But why?" Sampson asked.

"So, the person we are after could watch us in action."

"You mean to tell me he's here," Sampson said, looking around and ready to pounce.

"He was here," Donatella said placing a hand on his arm. "I'm pretty sure he's gone by now."

"So, he kidnapped Browning to draw us here so he could see us in action? But why?"

"Why indeed," she said looking back at the Demon's Breath ride. "Why indeed."

19

The FBI field office was a flurry of activities with the announcement of Special Agent Browning's abduction. Lawson turned over the search and recovery of the agent to her second in command, Anthony Adams. Adams transferred to the Charlotte field office from Chicago and was eager to make his mark. Keeping him busy with this meaningful activity gave her the leeway she needed to speak with The Syndicate operatives.

Vernon sent correspondence to Lawson advising and update was forthcoming from the team. With the morning's crisis, she decided to hold the conversation in the morning versus the lunch meeting they had previously scheduled. Both Jamison and Atwood had the morning off, so the meeting was delayed until they arrived at the office.

Jamison was first to speak once the group was settled. "What the hell's going on with 77? I had to take the surface streets just to get in here today."

"Shoot up on the highway," Rudolph said dispassionately, "and one of our quote-unquote own went missing.

But nothing for us to worry about. We have bigger fish to fry. What happened the other night?"

Jamison raised an eyebrow but continued, "I've never seen anything like it. I managed to follow King, undetected, to Hestia, where she seemed to be content to have a drink by herself. The night took a drastic and ultimately deadly turn when an unidentified male decided to pursue her. Seems like she made an impulsive decision to leave with him, and for a moment I lost contact. I was able to track them to his car, where they made out in the back. That is until she handed him a container of sorts. He sprayed something in his mouth, and within two minutes she was out of the car, and he was deceased in the back."

Rudolph, the resident IT Director, chimed in, "The victim's name is Trevor Collins. Married with one kid and by all accounts a successful real estate broker. Initial tox screen has comeback as an unknown compound, and authorities are suspecting foul play. Funny thing, when they went to pull footage from the countless cameras in and around the scene, they'd all been wiped clean."

"Some guardian angel," Atwood said after she finished off the last of her coffee.

Some guardian angel indeed, Lawson thought.

"I'll discreetly monitor the MEs findings to see if any light can be shed on the mysterious nature of his death."

"So, what gives, boss?" Jamison asked. "Are we still surveilling Mrs. King? And if so, is there anything more you can divulge about why?"

Lawson's phone vibrated on the tabletop. She answered and listened to the monolog on the other end of the line. Silence filled the room as the one-sided call continued until the agent responded, "Understood. We'll take care of it, and

I'll update you as soon as I have more information." She disconnected the call and addressed the group.

"It appears our missing agent has been rescued by none other than Special Agent Dabria. In doing so, it appears there were a few arrests made by the local PD. Those arrest were of Syndicate extended personnel. There were no sanctioned operations they should have been involved in, and of course we can't have them talking."

"I'm on it," Rudolph said, directing his attention back to his laptop. "I'll put in a transfer request to turn them over to the FBI."

"Atwood and I will go pick them up," Agent Vernon said. "We'll get the answers we need, and they'll quietly disappear."

Lawson interrupted, "Take Jamison instead. Atwood, I have a different assignment for you. It seems our colleague Donatella has requested a guard to be posted outside the room of Agent Browning. She appears to be concerned for her continued safety. I want you to be that agent. Find out what you can, why the agent was taken, why Donatella feels she may be in additional danger, and how this all ties back to The Syndicate."

Atwood nodded, and Lawson said, "Dismissed."

One by one, they exited Lawson's office until she was the lone occupant. She thumbed her contact list until she located the number for the head of The Syndicate, Susan. It rung twice before she answered, "I finished the morning debrief with the team. It seems Mrs. Veronica King has been a busy little bee. She killed a man at the bar with an unknown liquid compound. We are still looking into exactly what that was. And interestingly enough, there is no footage of the crime from all the surveillance equipment in the area."

She listened for a moment and then said, "My thoughts exactly. I'll pay Molly a visit later this afternoon."

THE TORRENTIAL DOWNPOUR that dominated most of the morning ended, and on the heels of it came the stifling humidity. When Sal was younger, he always snickered behind his father's back for carrying a handkerchief, commenting on how it made him look like an old man. Yet the relentless heat in this part of North Carolina mixed with the oppressive humidity caused him to reach in his back pocket, extract the monogrammed hanky, and mop his brows.

"Somebody forgot to tell Mother Nature to give us a break," Sal said, folding the handkerchief in half and wiping the sweat running down the side of his face.

"Oh, quit your bellyaching, you big baby," Jane admonished. "I'll make some iced tea when we're back home. In the meantime, get your game face on and let's meet with Emma. And let me do the talking."

"Why?"

"Because she's a girl who's lost her sister and brother in rapid succession. This interaction needs a gentle touch."

"Oh, I can be gentle," Sal said, reaching up to wipe away the perspiration once again.

Jane chuckled, "Oh, sugar bear, you're about as gentle as an F5 tornado to a house of cards. And besides, I didn't marry you because you're gentle. I married you because you're my gruff, rugged man."

She leaned over and kissed him on the cheek. As she turned toward the door, he mumbled under his breath, "I can be gentle."

Jane pressed the button on the Ring doorbell and patiently waited for their unannounced visit to be answered. She wondered if somewhere in the house Emma was evaluating them and determining if she was going to answer the door. Her question was answered when she heard the deadbolt being disengaged.

"Can I help you?" the mousy-voiced, bedraggled woman asked, keeping the door between the visitors and herself.

"We're looking for Emma Porter," Jane stated. "Are you her?"

She watched the woman consider being dishonest before saying, "I am. How can I help you?"

"My name is Jane. This is my husband Sal. I'm a retired journalist, and he's still active."

The skepticism began to etch on her face, but Jane continued. "We're not here about a story. We're here because of what happened to your sister, Elise. We also heard what happened to Edward, and on both accounts we want to offer our condolences."

"Thank you," she said, still uncommitted to her next course of action.

"We're friends of Detective Carl Sampson, your sister's partner. We're unofficially conducting our journalistic investigation to determine if we can provide some nugget of information that will bring her killer to justice."

Her eyes softened, and the rigidity in her body dissipated. "Please come in," she said opening the door and stepping to the side. Jane was first through the door followed by Sal. Emma closed and locked the door behind them. "Right this way."

The house was small but well maintained. Sunlight shone through the windows, illuminating the path to the family room. "Please take a seat. Can I offer you something to drink?"

"No, thank you," they answered in unison.

Emma positioned herself in the chair and without preamble launched into a story.

"Elise and Edward were always close. They had a bond that was unlike anything I ever shared with either of them. Honestly, at times I felt like the third wheel. But it's not like they didn't love me or care for me. It's just... Their bond was different. Tighter."

She wiped a tear from her eye with the back of her hand.

"She was always so protective of him too. It's no surprise to me that she went into law enforcement. It was in her nature to stick up for the little guy. When Edward was committed into the mental institution, they lost some of that closeness, and I think that started to tear her apart. But she never forgot about him. Not for one minute."

She abruptly stopped, turned to her side table, and retrieved a folder.

"Eddy was special in his own right. He was quiet and pretty much stayed to himself. But he was supremely talented." She opened the folder and extracted several sheets of paper. She lovingly gazed at the first one before passing it along to Jane.

"He had a keen eye for detail and could draw an exact replica of what his eyes took in. Before he was committed, he drew all the time, and Elise told him he needed to sign his artwork. He wasn't too keen on signing Edward, so he initialed each piece EP with the date in the bottom right-hand corner." She passed along a second and then a third. When she came to the fourth, she smiled and then passed it along to Jane.

She watched in silence as Jane took in the picture, not sure what to say. As the picture was passed along to Sal, his expression turned to curiosity as he too tried to make out the picture. Emma laughed out loud and then let them in on what they were looking at.

"Eddy also suffered from an extremely rare brain condition known as spatial orientation phenomenon."

Jane and Sal looked at each other, unsure what to say.

"Don't worry, many people haven't heard of it. Heck, until the doctor diagnosed Eddy, we had never heard of it either. In essence, those who suffer from this condition see the world upside down. The vast majority of those dealing with this condition see everything this way, but not Eddy. It seems as if his would come and go. It was never proven, but it seemed that he suffered from this most often when looking at faces. It didn't happen all the time, but when it did, he took a mental snapshot of the person he saw and then drew their likeness, as he saw it. So, if you flip the picture upside down, it'll make more sense to you."

Sal, who held the picture in his hand, spun the picture, and instantly a drawing of a man appeared.

"I've never seen this person before, but in the last few months, Eddy came across him, and he left an indelible mark on my little brother."

Jane took in the picture and had to stifle a gasp. The drawing was pure perfection when seen as intended. The exquisite detail, the shading, and not to mention the background scenery. All of it perfectly captured.

"I've never seen anything like this before," Jane said. "It's truly amazing. I know this is going to sound crazy, but could we possibly purchase this drawing from you? I'm sure it'll be impossible for me to retell this amazing story without having the genuine artifact there with me. And as mentioned, this isn't for any type of story. This would be for my own personal use."

Emma seemed taken aback by the request and finally said, "I've never once considered selling his work. You two seem like nice folks, so I'll let you have it. He's created many like that one."

"That's very kind of you," Jane said. "And we've taken up enough of your time today. We appreciate you spending some time chatting with us."

"Thank you for stopping by. I'm not sure I was much help, but I truly hope you find who killed my sister."

They exchanged their goodbyes, and Emma walked them to the door. They were both silent as they walked to the car, and Sal said, "Quick thinking. I'm glad you noticed what I did."

"It would have been impossible not to have noticed. As I said, the detail is uncanny."

"Indeed, it is," he said turning the drawing upside down once again and staring at it. "Now the question is, why was Troy Evans visiting Detective Porter's brother at the mental institution?"

"I don't know, but he certainly has some explaining to do."

20

Troy Evans sat in his home office staring at his computer with a splitting headache. His thoughts continued to replay how he'd arrived at this position. Moving to Charlotte was meant to be a new start for both him and Bethany. They were expecting a new child, they were turning their house into a home, and he had a new teaching job that within a few years allowed him to become tenured. Everything had been going well until she entered his class.

Mandy Cox was a second-year student at UNCC and had signed up for his creative writing class, the second in the series. There she sat in the center of the room, begging to be the center of attention. Prim, proper, blonde, and without a care in the world. Just like "her." He hadn't thought about "her" in years, and it would have stayed that way. But just like "her," Mandy thought the world was at her beck and call. She too thought she could manipulate people into doing what she wanted. This was evident in the way she had Hugo Wolfe wrapped around her finger, something she tried to do with him as well, and it came at her detriment.

The urge to address the Mandy situation had begun subsiding until Troy sat down to write his first thriller novel, deciding to step away from his previous genre and challenge himself with this one. Crafting the story had been therapeutic for Troy as his main character, Dillon, could embody the traits Troy felt he lacked. Where Troy straddled the fence, Dillon was decisive. Where Troy was meek and passive, Dillon was sure and assertive.

The more life Troy breathed into Dillon, the more he wanted to feel the confidence and power that he felt. When Dillon set out to stalk the women who were doing wrong in society, Troy decided he could do it too. And he knew who he could start with.

Troy and Dillon began to live parallel existences. For every action he took in the book, Troy took one in real life, all the way from the method of abduction to the killing blow of Mandy Cox. It had been so exhilarating and liberating, like when he had to get rid of "her" and the landlord. She had to go, and so did Mandy Cox.

Troy hesitated about the publication of his first book, *The Binds that Tie*, but once he decided on using a pseudonym instead of his real name, the apprehension went away. It took a little while to gain traction, but the readers, his fans, were clamoring for more. He'd give them more as the next victim he and Dillon began to stalk had already been determined prior to the conclusion of the first book.

It was around this time that the voice in his head became ever-present. He had been there before, but as Troy began penning his novels, the voice spoke louder and became more demanding. It had been the voice's suggestion to start the cat and mouse game with Detective Sampson.

The voice convinced Troy he could outsmart the detective. It was the voice that suggested leaving clues for Sampson to find the girl, Brianna Armstrong. And like in the first novel, Dillon mimicked these actions. Unfortunately, Sampson and the book's detective failed, and this marked another win for Troy. Again, the publication of his second book, *The Binds that Restrain*, obtained great success, and his fan following grew. But the voice wanted a challenge that couldn't be met by mere coeds. What fun was it to hunt someone who really couldn't put up a sporting fight?

Then entered Detective Elise Porter. Troy fought against going after her because she didn't exhibit the traits that made the other girls candidates. But the voice demanded it be her because she would be a worthy prey. In the end, Porter met the same fate as the other two, and Troy could feel the rush of adrenaline in achieving the goal.

Troy unlocked the bottom drawer of his desk and retrieved a set of books. He lovingly caressed the spine of each one, *The Binds that Tie, The Binds that Restrain, and The Binds that Imprison*. In a sense, they acted as his trophies from his three conquests. He sat the books on his desk and rubbed once again at his temples. The frequency and magnitude of his headaches were increasing, and today had been one of the worst.

Troy had been conflicted as the voice pushed him toward their next victim, ensuring it would bring them to heights never imagined. Going after Detective Porter had been one thing, but going after this next prey would be suicidal. But the voice wasn't hearing any of it. In fact, the voice reminded him at each turn that Dillon wouldn't second guess this decision. He would simply execute his plan and be home in time for the eleven o'clock news.

Troy devised a plan, one that he already set in motion, but his apprehension continued to grow. He looked back at his computer screen, where he'd been typing the final chapter in his fourth book. The final chapter was normally written after the victim had been taken care of, but Troy took a different approach for this novel.

In the beginning, the odds for success were small and continued to shrink by the day. So Troy made an executive decision and created two endings. One he planned to submit with the finished manuscript saw the tables being turned on Dillon and him not making it out alive. If somehow he succeeded in reaching the goal set out by the voice, he'd upload the manuscript with the alternate ending, the one that saw Dillon come out on top.

He clicked submit to upload his manuscript and set book number four, *The Binds that Obstruct*, available for pre-order. The voice came barging in on his thoughts. *And what about Beth? She's blonde now. She's one of them. She must be dealt with.*

"Go away, dammit!" he screamed as he pounded the heal of his hand against his forehead. He winced at the pain, squeezing his eyes tight to push both the voice and the pain away.

A knock came at the door. "Is everything okay," Beth asked, bringing him back to the present. He hurried to put the books away in the drawer as she walked in.

"Yeah. I'm okay. I have a splitting headache. Do we have any pain medicine?"

"No, I'm sorry, hon. I took the last two pills the other day. I can go to the store and get some."

Look at that blonde hair. Do something about her like you did for Mandy, Brianna, and your mom. Troy ignored the voice and said, "That's okay. I could use some fresh air anyway. I'll go get some. Is there anything you need from the store?"

"Only a few items. Can I send you a list?"

"You know it. But before I go, why don't I go up and give Emily a big hug?"

Beth smiled. "I'm sure she'd like that. But I hope I'm on the list for a hug as well."

He stood and walked over to her. "Of course you are, my dear. It goes without saying." He pulled her in for a long embrace, holding on a few extra beats.

21

Special Agent in Charge Jessica Lawson spent little time at The Syndicate headquarters and much less since she took over the helm within the FBI. Nonetheless, she felt slightly embarrassed she needed to request directions to the IT department. She could only recall one instance she paid a visit to the department, and that was to obtain her company issued devices.

She'd had numerous interactions with Molly Jenkins, the company's uber nerd, mostly over her various technologies. Today wouldn't be a social call nor an issue with her devices. She had questions for Molly, and Lawson hoped for the young girl's sake the answers were ... sufficient.

The elevator doors opened, and Lawson took the left in search of the Honeycomb area, as dubbed by the IT team. Its name was derived from the desk configuration deployed on the floor, and Molly was considered the queen of the hive. Finding the open room concept was quick, and locating Molly's location was even quicker, since hers was the one with a crown adorning the station.

She noted Molly's head bobbing rhythmically to the music playing from her over-the-ear headphones. She approached undetected and tapped Molly on her shoulder.

The action startled her, as she turned and recognized her visitor. "Ms. Lawson, everything okay with your equipment? You know, if you had an issue, you could have given me a call and I could have come to you."

Lawson gave her a disarming smile. "No, all is well with my equipment. And again, thank you for the upgrades. They are working better than expected. But I do have a few questions for you. Is there somewhere we can talk in private?"

Molly furrowed her brows and then said, "Sure, right this way." She sprang from her seat, heading in the opposite direction from where Lawson had entered. Molly found the room she was searching for and ushered Lawson in. "Please take a seat," she said, closing the door behind them. Lawson found a chair and noticed Molly push a button on the wall. The window looking out onto the floor darkened, but it didn't obscure her vision.

"Privacy window," Molly said, answering the unasked question. "It allows us to see out, but those on the outside cannot see in. It also set the room to occupied on the tablet outside the door. So what can I do for you today?"

"Ms. Jenkins, we had a curious incident happen at Ballantyne Village that I'm hoping you can shed some light on. You see, a murder, and from what I'm told a gruesome one, was perpetrated there, yet authorities are stymied because video footage of the crime seems to have been expertly scrubbed from all surrounding surveillance footage. While I'm sure there are some hackers who could pull off this feat, I've never known anyone to be more thorough than you are. Is there anything you'd like to share?"

Lawson sat back in her chair, letting the silence build, but she didn't need to wait long.

"I received a call from Ms. King on the night in question. She instructed me to remove the footage from Hestia and everything within a three-block radius, including home footage. In the last job I ran with Ms. King, I sabotaged the comms, for which Ms. Yates paid me a visit. She made it clear I was not to do anything like that again. When Ms. King made her request, I figured it was a sanctioned job, and knowing the trouble I was in from disobeying an order last time, I did as I was asked. Was I wrong in doing so?"

Lawson didn't answer the question. Instead, she asked one of her own. "Did you make a copy of the footage prior to deleting it?" Molly squirmed in her seat. When a request to scrub data was made, there were to be no copies left of it, no exceptions. "In this case, if you did, it'll go a long way toward your redemption."

The wheels were turning in the young genius's mind until she said, "Yes, I have a copy."

"Good. Now, if you don't mind, send me a copy of the footage that traces the path of Ms. King from the rooftop down to the parking garage to my phone." She stood to exit and before walking out the door, she said, "Molly, be more careful when being asked to clear data of someone's mess. It would be a shame if one of the worker bees had to clear video footage involving you."

SUSAN YATES GREW up with the belief that she was different than her classmates. She was a straight-A student for whom academic studies came easily. She was a middle-of-the-pack athlete, though for her it wasn't about the games and the outcome. For Susan, it was all about the strategy and how to anticipate what the other person was going to do and counteract their move before they ever started to make it. She also had a way with people that some considered manipulative, but she considered them win-win opportunities. Every person you encountered intrinsically expected a transaction. She simply found a way to ensure her transactions were met while providing one of significantly less value to the other person.

She parlayed her skills to several full ride scholarships to the schools of her choice. Ultimately, she selected one with a bustling student population. Because for Susan, college wasn't about getting a degree but instead an opportunity to observe human nature when left relatively unsupervised. Her peers became case studies, and her professors, well they were unwitting adversaries in games that they were completely unaware they were playing.

Like grade school, and high school, her college studies came to her easily. As a result, it left plenty of time for her to engage in extra-curricular activities, some of which connected her with less than desirable crowds that made Susan feel right at home. These crowds led to her current station in life atop The Syndicate, an organization that allowed her to utilize the skills she spent a lifetime honing.

She stared from the floor-to-ceiling windows in her corner office at The Syndicate's headquarters. The city hadn't experienced a thunderstorm of that ferocity since Hurricane Hugo. Yet somehow the storms brought her a sense of calm. However, her calm state was systematically being destroyed as the last words from her visitor faded into the background.

Spencer had been one of her finest recruits. A brilliant strategist, an unmatched tactician, and as loyal as they came. And yet with those attributes he still managed to run a mission, in the city, that was bringing unneeded attention from the authorities. As if the shootout in rush hour traffic on one of Charlottes busiest interstates wasn't enough, he ordered his men to kidnap an FBI agent.

What infuriated Susan more than the operation was from whom he received the directive, Veronica King. Susan was preparing to ask about the man he'd been advised to work for when there was a knock at the door.

"Enter."

The door opened, and SAIC Lawson walked into the office.

"I'll be right with you," Susan said, acknowledging her newest visitor. She faced Spencer. "You're dismissed." A relieved expression colored his face as he stood to leave.

Once he exited and closed the door behind him, Susan buzzed her executive admin. "Please send a cleaning crew to Spencer's house, and advise them to stay on site until he arrives. Allow him to walk in and feel the devastation he created, and then add him to the trash. After, contact Elliot and have him come see me. It appears he has been promoted, and I want him to fully understand his duties."

She turned back to Lawson and said, "What do you have for me?"

"I've already updated you on the latest surveillance of Veronica King. I paid a visit to Molly this afternoon and obtained the footage that had been wiped." Susan raised an eyebrow. "She's been given a pass for maintaining the data this time, and I made it clear she is operating on thin ice."

Susan nodded, and Lawson continued, "Take a look at this." She handed over her phone and watched the expressionless façade as Susan watched the video. When it concluded, Lawson continued, "I don't know what game she's playing, but it appears she's up to something. What would you like for us to do next?"

Susan sat silent for a minute and then said, "Don't do a thing. Your team has done well, and you can call off the surveillance. I've been at this game much longer than she has, and she's beginning to telegraph her next steps without even realizing it."

Susan pulled her pen from the holder and extracted paper from the drawer in her desk. She scribbled a few lines on it and handed it over to Lawson. "See if you can find more information about this man. It seems Veronica instructed Spencer and his crew to do work for him. I'd like to know why."

"You've got it." She started to ask if there was anything else when her phone vibrated. She looked down and read the two-word text from Cole Vernon, "Job done." Lawson instead said, "The crew arrested by the police has been dealt with."

"Excellent, now find this mystery man."

"Will do," Lawson said before exiting the office. Once Susan was again alone in her office with her thoughts, she simply said, "Checkers vs chess. May the better woman win."

22

Dusk had settled over the city when Bethany awoke from her nap. She squeezed one in at every opportunity, because having an infant was more work than she imagined. She often wondered why her mom didn't tell her it was this hard, but who was she kidding? It wouldn't have made a difference, because having Emily brought her infinite amounts of happiness.

Troy must have seen her asleep on the couch and decided not to wake her. He'd always been so considerate. Then she recalled the headache he mentioned earlier and him heading out to the store. *I'll go check in on him and see what he wants for dinner,* she thought as she shifted to a seated position on the couch. She was in the mood for Thai or maybe even a burger. As she approached the office, she admitted to herself that she could eat anything at this point as long as it was hot.

She knocked but didn't hear any sound coming from inside. She opened the door. "Hey, hon, how's that headache?" She was surprised to find his office empty. She noticed the reflective glare from the monitor shining on the window. *Maybe he was in the bathroom or checking in on Emily.* She decided she'd hang out in the office until he returned.

Five minutes passed before she gave up, and in an effort to save electricity she decided to turn off his laptop and monitor. She ran her finger across the trackpad in search of the shut down command. Her finger hovered above the pad, ready to click, when the words "FBI Agent" stood out on the word document. *Maybe a paper from a student*, she thought until she noticed the word count down in the corner, 43,498. Clearly not a student's paper.

Curiosity growing, she began to read more. It finally hit her that this was a draft of a novel. She read on, becoming more concerned with what she was reading. *Did Troy write this?* She backed away from the screen when she noticed the bottom drawer askew. She pulled it open to find three novels by William Stealth. *The Binds that Tie, The Binds that Restrain, and The Binds that Imprison.* Physical books weren't Troy's thing, so the fact he had three by the same author was shocking. His reading typically came in the form of audiobooks in the fantasy genre.

She cracked open *The Binds that Tie* to a random chapter and began to read. As she did, the story felt vaguely familiar. Her eyes flew over the words line by line while her brain processed their meaning. She gasped with the realization that the story mimicked the description of what happened to Mandy, the first victim in the case Donatella and Sampson were working.

She picked up the second book, *The Binds that Restrain,* and began to read. She skimmed the first chapter looking for something familiar but didn't find anything. She moved along to the second chapter, and finding nothing of note, she began to breathe a sigh of relieve. She decided to skim one additional chapter, and a third of the way through she found it. The break-in and abduction, both similar to what she recalled from the news regarding the second victim.

She dropped it and picked up the final book, *The Binds that Imprison*. She instantly flipped to the end of the book, as the coverage for what happened to Detective Porter dominated the news cycle for over a week. Two pages in, her fears were realized. This book told the story of Detective Porter's abduction and subsequent murder. Her fingers went numb as the book slid from her fingers. *Why would Troy have these books?* she wondered when a frightening thought crossed her mind.

"No!" she said in a mumble as her breaths grew shallow.

She turned back to the laptop, fingers trembling, mind racing. She dragged the bar back to the beginning of the Word document.

"No!" she screamed at the top of her lungs as she read:
The Binds that Confine
Written By: William Stealth

"Who's a good boy?" Jasmyn asked Sebastian while holding mash peas on a spoon for him to eat. She resorted to making airplane noises as she guided the spoon toward his mouth. Once again, he turned his head, defiantly refusing to take a bite.

"Sebastian, you need to eat your vegetables if you want to grow to be big and strong." She was giving it another go when the doorbell rang, which brought a smile to his face.

"Saved by the bell, mister. But this isn't over," she said, smiling and placing the spoon on his tray. She wiped her hands and scurried to the door.

"Sal, Jane, what a surprise."

"We're sorry to drop by unannounced, but we wondered if we could ask you a couple of questions."

"Absolutely. Please come in. Sebastian is finishing up his dinner. Please have a seat."

The Grandsons headed to the family room, and Jasmyn went back into the kitchen. There the picture told the story of what transpired from the time she left.

Sebastian's plate no longer consisted of mashed peas, only mashed potatoes. Maggie, their dog, was guiltily licking her lips. And Sebastian was working a spoon full of mashed potatoes to his mouth. It took a couple of minutes for him to finish feeding himself. "Good job, honey," Jasmyn said, wiping his mouth while removing the tray from the highchair. She smiled then said, "And for the record, I know what you did. Tomorrow, it's greens. I'm going to keep my eye on you."

She finished cleaning him up and headed into the family room. Marcellous rounded the corner after coming downstairs as Jane outstretched her arms for Sebastian. "Who's your favorite auntie," she asked snuggling him which caused him to giggle.

"Sal, Jane. I didn't know you guys were here. No please, keep your seat," Marcellous said as Sal prepared to stand and greet him.

"It's an unscheduled visit," Sal said, "and we do apologize for dropping in like this, but something has come up that's time sensitive. It could be nothing, but then again it could be something."

"Consider our curiosity piqued with that cryptic statement," Marcellous said.

Sal continued, "Jasmyn, you met Beth at your OB's office, correct?"

"Yes, she was new and looked like she was having a rough go of things. We struck up a conversation and bonded over the birth of our first deliveries. It was refreshing to have a new so to be mother to share in the pregnancy experience."

"When did you first meet Troy?"

"Well, let me think. I'm pretty certain it was, yeah, it was at our dinner party before the babies were born. Wait, are you planning to write a story on them? I want to know all the juicy details."

"Not exactly," Jane stepped in while balancing Sebastian on her knee. "From your interactions with him, what's your take on Troy?"

"He's quiet, for sure. That's one of the things Beth told me about him before we met. She said he can be introspective, observant, and extremely bright. She said he doesn't like to talk about it, but he has an IQ of 146."

Jane and Sal looked at each other.

"Come on, guys," Marcellous said. "What's this all about?"

"Jane and I have taken an interest in the case Sampson and Donatella are working. We, um, wanted to see if we could do some investigative journalism and find something that could help."

"Sal found that Detective Porter had a brother, Edward, locked away in a mental institution. We went to pay him a visit only to find out that he had passed away."

"That's terrible," Jasmyn said. "That poor family."

"Jane worked her magic, and we found that they had a younger sister, Emma. We secured an address and paid her a visit."

"I took the lead throughout the conversation because you know how gruff Sal can be."

Jasmyn nodded, which garnered a glare from Sal.

"As you can imagine, she was heartbroken. She told us about the closeness of her siblings and the skills they both had. It turns out that Edward's hidden talent was art. He had what I would call perfect recall. He see a scene in front of him and could redraw it from memory exactly as he saw it."

Sal reached into the folder he'd been carrying and extracted a piece of paper that he then handed to Jasmyn. He said, "He suffered from a condition known as spatial orientation phenomenon."

"I've heard of that," Marcellous said, shocking everyone sitting around the family room. "I was doing some research about a year back and came across the term. It's a condition in which the person sees the world upside down."

"Correct you are, Mr. Thompson," Jane said. "Edward's condition was acute. He only saw faces in this manner, and it wasn't all the time. But each time he did, he would draw the person he saw."

"That's fascinating and all, but what does this have to do with Beth and Troy?" Jasmyn asked.

Jane hesitated and then said, "Maybe nothing or maybe something. We aren't sure. But please go ahead and flip the drawing in your hand upside down."

Jasmyn gave the universal sign of bewilderment, head tilted to the side, eyes squinting. Nonetheless, she did what was asked, Marcellous looking over her shoulder. With the picture completely upside down, her wide eyes gave away the recognition.

"Is that...Troy? It can't be. I mean, how? Why?"

"We have the same questions," Sal commented. "It's clear he visited Edward, someone we didn't even know existed until last night."

Suddenly the doorbell rang repeatedly with increased urgency, followed by an insistent knock on the door.

"What in the world?" Jasmyn said as Marcellous went through the foyer. Shortly after he had the door opened, the sound of rapid footsteps could be heard echoing from the foyer.

Beth entered, eyes bloodshot red, tears streaming down her cheeks, carrying her daughter in one arm while holding a bag in the other. "Oh my God. I think it's him. I think it's Troy."

23

Sal and Jasmyn rushed to Bethany's aid, as she looked to be on the verge of a breakdown. Jasmyn took Emily from her arms while Sal helped her to the sofa. Jasmyn sat Emily next to Jane, who was still holding Sebastian. Marcellous went to the refrigerator, extracted a bottle of water, twisted off the cap, and handed it to Jasmyn, who in turn handed it to Beth.

"Here, drink this and tell us what happened."

Beth's eyes were wild as she drank from the bottle. Her voice trembled as she spoke, "I awoke after falling asleep on the couch. I'd been so tired after the long day Emily and I spent together. She was down for a nap, so I sat down to read a book , but my body had different plans. Prior to that, I thought I heard Troy talking to someone in his office, but I was wrong. When I went to check on him, he said he had a headache and was going to go grab some medicine from the store. That's when I decided to read until he returned."

She took another drink and continued, "As I said, I must have fallen asleep, because when I awoke it was getting dark outside. I went to his office to check on him, but he wasn't there. I noticed his monitor was still on, so I went to turn it off. When I did..." She broke down into tears and uncontrollable sobbing.

Jasmyn stroked her trembling hands. "It's okay. Take your time."

Bethany let out a heavy sigh. "When I did, the words 'FBI Agent' stood out on the screen. I read a few words thinking it was a story from one of his students. I then noticed a partially open drawer at the bottom of his desk, and I found these." She patted the bag sitting on her lap.

She placed the water on the ground next to her and retrieved the contents. Jasmyn took the offered items, realizing they were paperback books. "I've been married to Troy for years, and we dated long before that. In that time, the only books I ever saw him read were textbooks. So I found it strange he had fiction novels, especially by the same author."

Jasmyn rotated the books so she could see the spine and silently read the titles. Bethany continued, "I cracked one open and read a little bit then did the same with the second and third. That's when I realized each of the books were a retelling of murders that had been in the news. The murders of Mandy Cox, Brianna Armstrong, and..." She tapped her foot as she willed herself to say the last name. "And the murder of Detective Porter." She began wringing her hands before interlacing her fingers beneath her nose.

"My mind was racing, because for the life of me I couldn't understand why Troy, my husband, would have books that detailed the murders of those poor women. I wasn't even sure how he'd come across them. Worse, what sick monster would write books about what happened to those women?" she said, bowing her head into her interlaced fingers, tears streaming again. "I thought back to the story on the computer. I scrolled back to the beginning to find it was written by the same author of those three books. The author may say William Stealth, but the man behind that name is...Troy."

She broke down into tears again. The room grew silent as they processed this bombshell that Bethany dropped on them.

Sal gasped. "I think we need to Call Donatella and Sampson."

"No! We can't," Bethany hastened.

"Sal's right. We need to contact them," Jasmyn said, squeezing Beth's hand.

After contemplating the statement, Bethany slowly nodded and whispered, "Okay."

SPECIAL AGENT DABRIA and Detective Sampson were on the other side of town working the case. As a result, it took them thirty minutes to arrive after Jasmyn's urgent request. She brought them into the family room, where Sebastian and Emily were playing in the playpen. Marcellous was brewing coffee while Jane and Sal comforted Bethany, who was still obviously shaken. She retold the story to the newcomers, breaking down once again as she reached the conclusion. Sal and Jane added the information they uncovered from their visit with Detective Porter's sister and handed over the picture that had been drawn by Edward.

"Where is he now?" Donatella asked as she felt Sampson fuming next to her.

"I don't know. I haven't seen him since he left for the pharmacy."

Donatella pulled her phone from her pocket and called BJ. "I need you to trace the whereabouts of Troy Evans." She recited the number from memory, causing a look of confusion from Bethany. She eyed the distraught woman as she awaited BJ's reply with a mixture of empathy and disbelief.

It was clear her emotions were genuine verging on the state of shock. The Thompsons and Grandsons were doing everything possible to comfort her. Donatella had witnessed scenes like this before, and Bethany was holding on by the thinnest of strings.

On the flip side of the coin, she found it hard to believe there were no signs. Keeping a secret this big required a tremendous amount of compartmentalization. And no matter how good you were at it, you were bound to slip a time or two. The true question was if anyone would notice the slip.

BJ returned, and she listened intently. "Thank you. And stay close, I suspect we'll need your assistance before this night is over."

She disconnected the call, turned to Sampson, and said, "He's Uptown. We better go." She was already on the move, and he was preparing to follow.

"Wait," a voice called from behind them. "Please, wait. I know you have a job to do, but I beg of you to please spare his life. He has a daughter who loves him, and I know he loves her. I don't know. I don't want him to die. Please."

"Bethany," Donatella said in her firm southern drawl, "if he comes in peacefully, he has nothing to worry about.

But if he puts up a fight or puts anyone else's life in danger, it's our job to protect them first and ourselves second."

With the matter closed, Donatella and Sampson continued to the door, intent on bringing this ordeal to an end.

24

The city of Charlotte poured millions upon millions of dollars into the uptown area with the goal of building the night life in the center of the city. Infrastructure played a vital role as a new trolley system was introduced to allow easy transportation. This reduced the risk of driving drunk and at the same time encouraged those who took the public transportation to drink more.

Trendy housing that catered to millennials was next on the docket. Access to the heart of the city by simply walking out of your front door appealed to this group. Living in these condos and apartments came at a premium, but it also afforded the night life coveted by this age bracket.

Cuisine of the highest quality attracted those who lived away from Uptown. A happening culinary scene was vital to the area's growth and would lead to sustained success.

Still, one of the major draws to any bustling areas was the different forms of entertainment, for which Uptown Charlotte wasn't lacking. They had sports teams for basketball, football, soccer, and semi-pro baseball, but concerts, especially outside concerts, drew in crowds like none other. If the concert was held at an open-air stadium, with tremendous acoustics, you too could enjoy the festivities by virtue of proximity.

Tonight, SZA was performing to a sold-out, standing-room-only crowd at the Knights' baseball stadium, Truist Field. Those who couldn't secure tickets were camping outside of the stadium, while those who lived in the buildings that overlooked the stadium simply brought lawn chairs on their balconies and settled in for the evening.

A police presence was visible but not overbearing. They were there to keep the peace but not to impede fun. If the fun didn't get too far out of hand, they allowed many things to slide. They were also reminding girls of all ages to be mindful of their surroundings. Inside the department, this maniac was being elevated to that of a serial killer. They didn't want to alarm the city and didn't publicly refer to him as such, but they wanted to keep the citizens they swore to protect as safe as possible.

Troy Evans waved to an officer as he continued meandering past Truist Field. He was keenly aware what was nearby, since it followed his plan, but he was still fuzzy on how he arrived at this location. The last thing he recalled was leaving the house in search of migraine medicine and then regaining consciousness in an uptown parking garage.

A concert for an artist he was unfamiliar with was underway, and yet he found himself captivated by the rhythm of the beat. He wasn't sure why he'd been drawn here today, but the inner voice was at the wheel dictating every move he made.

He smiled disingenuously and waved as he passed

another officer. He wanted to give all appearances that everything was fine, even though he felt far from that being the case. With his body movements on autopilot, he ran through his plan, once again looking for any holes. He reminded himself that the key to conquering this prey was in misdirection and ingenuity.

Abruptly he stopped, slid to his left to move from the flow of traffic, and simply waited. *It'll be clear in due time*, the voice said, answering the question that had been forming in his thoughts.

SPECIAL AGENT DABRIA and Detective Sampson exited her Audi R8 Spyder three blocks away from the Truist Field. She parked in a spot designated for law enforcement and displayed her credentials on the dash.

"The latest ping of his cell phone places him near this area," Donatella said as they began walking south on N. Church St. toward the concert. This had been the first thing spoken the entire ride. She began to wonder if Sampson was in the right headspace. To have your partner murdered by someone you recently unknowingly shared a meal with would be a lot to handle. Keeping this bottled inside could generate an explosion of anger at the wrong time.

"How are you doing?" she prodded.

"I'm good," he blurted out. "He'll be nearly impossible to spot in this crowd."

"Leave that to me," she said, quickly and expertly scanning every face in the crowd. BJ's tech had saved her life on many occasions, and though the contact lenses were new to her, she felt confident the facial recognition would do as the genius intended.

She continued, "With a crowd this size, we shouldn't pull our weapons unless absolutely necessary. Let's do our best to corner him without making a scene."

"Sure," he said noncommittally.

This garnered a glare from Donatella, which the detective simply ignored as he continued searching the crowd. She was turning away from Sampson when she received a notification ping from her phone. She reached in her pocket and read the notification on the display, *93% match*.

She stuck out a hand to stop Sampson's forward momentum while simultaneously looking past his shoulder. She squinted and then said, "Found him at your four o'clock."

SAIC JESSICA LAWSON, Special Agent Vernon, and Special Agent Jamison gathered at the corner of West 3rd St and South Tryon St. in Uptown Charlotte. After her meeting with Susan Yates, Lawson headed back to the FBI field office and went to work locating her mystery man.

The vehicle driven by Spencer to meet with his contact was Syndicate issued and equipped with video. Lawson requested that Molly pull the video and send it to her stat. Within five minutes of the request, Lawson received it in her inbox. She surmised the chat she had with the younger woman had something to do with the speed.

Lawson watched the video, searching for clues that would tell her who he was. He'd come to the meeting with a hat on that he wore low, which prevented her from obtaining a clear enough shot to run facial recognition. But toward the end of the conversation, as he headed back to his vehicle, he touched the light pole next to his parked car.

She contacted Vernon, who was still in the field with Jamison, and instructed them to visit the location and pull the print. She sent a copy of the video to him to reduce any confusion. The two of them were only twenty minutes away from the location. It took them five minutes to find the print in question and another twenty to arrive back at the field office.

Lawson ordered a priority run on the print, and within an hour of her receiving the video, she'd identified her subject, Troy Evans. She put Rudolph on the trail of finding his location, which he'd done by identifying his phone number and tracking his location. Instead of using cell towers to triangulate his location, Rudolph hacked into Troy's iPhone and activated Location Services. This provided his exact location utilizing GPS, which brought Lawson and the team to Uptown Charlotte.

The roads they needed to take were blocked off because of a concert, and while she could use her FBI credentials to force her way through, she didn't want to draw any attention to her or her team. Furthermore, they were tracking him via GPS, so there was no danger of losing him.

"Let's handle this quickly and quietly," Lawson said. "We need to know why he was directing a group of Syndicate members and what his connection is with Veronica King."

"I take it we won't be using any weapons," Jamison said, already sure of the answer.

"That's correct. Taking him alive is our best course of

action. Now, let's go. We can use the crowd as cover, so do your best to blend in."

They started down West 3rd, a straight shot to the stadium and where the GPS pinpointed Troy. They were approaching South Poplar Street when Jamison urged the group to stop.

"It's that Special Agent Dabria," he asked, nodding his head up and to the right of their location.

Vernon and Lawson turned their heads in the same direction.

"Appears so," Vernon said, "and she seems locked in on something, or someone."

Lawson's phone vibrated in her pocket. She checked the caller ID, noting it was Atwood on the other end. She answered, listening intently while the agent relayed new information.

"Thank you for the update. That's excellent work. I doubt we'll need you here. Call the switchboard and have them send someone out to replace you. While our surveillance of King has come to an end, I'd like you to find her whereabouts."

She disconnected the call and said, "Seems Agent Browning was creating a profile for Special Agent Dabria prior to her abduction. The profile is for the person responsible for the kidnapping and skinning of those two girls from the news in addition to the death of the police detective."

For the first time, Jamison noted the man walking with Donatella. "Speaking of which, I believe that's the slain detective's partner with Donatella."

"What are the odds?" Vernon asked, eyeing his phone. "It looks like they are headed in the direction of Mr. Evans."

"Let's stay back and observe," Lawson said, "There's more going on here. A lot more."

TROY WAS on the move once again, but this time he had a firm destination in mind. He knew the final destination but found it strange to be taking a circuitous route. He excused himself as he maneuvered through the assembled mass of people and varied his speeds when unimpeded.

He turned onto South Graham Street, where he spotted the building next to the luxurious Circa Uptown Apartments. He managed to purchase the building from a developer from California. They had plans to turn the space into townhomes but later backed out of the plans. This had become his pet project specifically tailored for one purpose, to ensnare his prey.

He had contractors working around the clock outfitting every inch of the building per his design. Contractors were paid handsomely under the table, because according to the city, this building was empty, undeveloped, and would not have any occupants. And most of this was true. It would not have any occupants, but it would play witness to a game between two strategists.

He admired the massive building as he made his final approach. He arrived at the front door, where he was confronted by a keypad. He entered the eight-digit code, and the deadbolt began to retract. He entered and slowly maneuvered the spring-loaded door to the latch that would keep it ajar. He quickly moved to his left and pulled the lever that revealed the hidden door that led to his control room. There he would be able to watch and alter events as he saw fit. This was the house of horrors that he created for Special Agent Donatella Dabria. There was no doubt that Detective Sampson would be in tow, and Troy had different plans for him.

He arrived at the room with the equipment already running. As he did, he saw two figures, Sampson and Donatella, approaching the outside of the building. After some conversation that he couldn't hear, they approached the front door. Sampson was the first one through, followed by Donatella.

He watched as the door closed and locked behind them and said, "Let the games begin."

WHEN DONATELLA SPOTTED TROY, he was standing in the shadow of the stadium staring off into the distance. Sampson was ready to move in, but Donatella advised patience as they observed him. She replayed the instructions from BJ to activate Tracking Mode. She quickly blinked her eyes three times before fixating on Troy. She then closed her eyes and counted to three before opening her eyes again.

She wasn't sure what to expect, but his body being outlined in a reddish-orange hue was not at the top of her guesses. She was pleasantly pleased to find her vision clear even in this tracking mode.

She continued to watch as he stood motionless as if in a trance or waiting on something to transpire. Without provocation, he snapped out of it and began walking in the opposite direction.

"Let's go," Donatella said, crossing the street and

keeping him in her visual plane.

"So what's the plan here?" Sampson asked, stepping aside to avoid being hit by a young girl dancing to the music.

"Ideally, we get him alone with no chance of collateral damage. And if not alone, I'd settle for a space sparsely populated."

"I wouldn't mind getting him alone," Sampson said through gritted teeth.

She knew it was his pain talking, and while a word of comfort may have helped, she refrained from saying what was in her heart. Instead, she said, "Let's not get ahead of ourselves. It's important we keep our minds clear."

Troy began to pick up the pace, which they were finding hard to match on this densely packed sidewalk.

The artist began singing one of her marquee songs, "Kill Bill," which brought the already hyper crowd into a frenzy. They stood in a haphazard unison with arms flailing and started singing along.

"We're losing him," Sampson said, displacing a few concertgoers out of his way as he tried to locate their subject.

Donatella shifted her direction thirty degrees to the left and said, "This way." Flickers of his heat signature danced periodically through cracks in the crowd. She quickly searched for a point of intersection and a clear path that would make trailing him easier. Finding none, she continued to push through the mob, being jostled along the way.

Another twenty seconds and they were through the heart of the crowd, and she caught a glimpse of Troy making a left at the next intersection. Sampson must have eyed the motion as he was already moving in that direction before Donatella could make mention of the next move.

This unexpected speed bump placed them further away from him than when they first started, but thanks to BJ's invention, he was still in the agent's sights.

As they turned the corner, they watched Troy enter a massive building on the right side of the street. Sampson picked up the pace, and Donatella followed suit.

When they arrived, they noticed the door partially open.

"Looks like we have an invitation," Sampson said, turning to Donatella.

"Yeah, and something doesn't feel quite right about this."

"We have to go in," Sampson said.

"Yes, we do, but keep your eyes open. There's no telling what he has in store."

Sampson nodded and proceeded to the entrance. He pushed and held it open so Donatella could follow in behind him. When he let it go, it swung back with a thud and a series of mechanical locks maneuvered into place, sealing them inside and away from the outside world.

JAMISON LED the team following Donatella and Sampson as they trailed Troy Evans. His blood lust for the special agent was something Lawson advised him to keep under control. His desire to erase her existence could cloud his judgment and one day cost him his life. But his ego stood firm in his belief that he could handle anything that came his way.

Lawson ran various scenarios through her head to deal

with the situation as it unfolded real-time. Her instructions were to find the mystery man, which she had done, but finding him would not be enough. They needed to understand his involvement with Veronica King. It was clear she was angling at something, but no one could figure out what. Having an opportunity to interrogate him would provide some answers.

The tangential connection between Troy and Donatella's case could prove troublesome. If he knew more than he should, he'd likely fold under questioning from Donatella. As much as she despised the woman, she could admit she was exceptional at her job. But now wasn't the time to laude over her intellectual prowess. She needed to decide on a course of action and do so quickly.

As Jamison continued to lead the party, Lawson realized the area was becoming more sparsely populated, and if she was going to act, she would need to do so soon. She was about to turn to Vernon to consult with him on a hastily made plan she had devised when she noticed Troy dip into an unmarked building.

This unexpected action caused Donatella and Sampson to pause outside the door, which caused Jamison to hold his team firm and out of viewing position. Lawson watched as they engaged in a conversation before obviously settling on a decision. She watched as they walked into the building and then made up her mind.

"Follow me. We're going in after them."

She sprinted across the street, followed by Jamison and Vernon. They brushed past bystanders singing along to the music and reached the door mere seconds after Donatella and Sampson entered. Her dismay was palpable when she realized the door was locked and required a digital code to enter.

"Spread out and look for a back or side entrance."

Jamison headed to the left, Vernon the right. Two minutes later, they both came jogging up the right side. Vernon said, "There isn't another entrance into this building. There appears to have been a back door at some point that has now been replaced with brick. We also checked all the ground floor windows, or at least that's what they should be. Upon closer inspection, behind each of them is a wall of concrete. What we are seeing is a façade. There's no telling what's behind that door."

Lawson began playing back everything she'd uncovered within the last hour. Troy was responsible for the carnage on I-77. He'd kidnapped an FBI agent and taken over an amusement park. He was being sought by Donatella and Sampson for potentially murdering those two coeds and a police detective. And now he'd lured them into a building with one entrance with God knows what behind the door.

"Retreat," she finally said after contemplation. "We'll hold up out of sight and see who emerges. If it's Troy, we apprehend him. If it's Donatella or Sampson, we pack it up and go home."

25

The clink of the doors locking behind them echoed in the vast open area. The minimal lighting cast ominous shadows in varying locations. Although they viewed windows on the ground floor from outside the building, the interior was void of natural lighting.

"Now what?" Sampson asked, searching the room for where to go next.

His question was answered when a single ding sounded directly in front of them. Elevator doors slid open, and the light from the elevator spilled into the walkway.

"I guess that's our answer," he said, taking the lead. Although the room appeared empty, they didn't take any chances. They carefully cleared every crevice as they proceeded toward the elevator.

They reached the elevator without incident and were confronted with buttons representing floors B to 16.

"Start at the top and work our way down," Donatella said, pressing 16.

As the doors closed, Sampson said, "Works for me."

The car shot up at Mach speed before abruptly coming to a stop. The juxtaposition of the doors slowly opening and the elevator car quickly rising was jarring.

"Floor 8," Sampson said, pointing at the placard. "I thought you pressed 16."

"I did," Donatella said, exiting the elevator, "but that's not our most pressing issue."

In front of them was a revolving door flanked by two brick walls. The door, reminiscent of a cylinder, only had enough room for one person to enter at a time, forcing the other person to wait. The dim lighting prevented them from seeing anything more than five feet in front of them.

The whoosh of the elevator doors closing cast them into further darkness. Sampson turned to push the button for the door to reopen only to find there wasn't one.

"Doesn't look like we have much of a choice but to press forward," she said.

"Wait a minute," Sampson said, placing an arm on her shoulder to hold her back, "we have no clue what's on the other side. And considering I got you into this, I should be the one to go first."

"By all means, after you, Detective," she said, stepping aside and ushering him past.

It took Sampson three steps to come face-to-face with the constantly spinning door. Even as he stood directly in front of it, he couldn't tell what was on the other side. With no hesitation, he stepped in.

Donatella watched as the door pushed him along. She waited for the opening to come back around, and as expected it was empty. She stepped in and thanked her lucky stars she was not claustrophobic. She had just enough room to shimmy along with absolutely no room to turn around in place.

When the door came to the opening on the other side, Sampson wasn't anywhere to be found. Instead, she found herself in a narrow corridor that doglegged to the left. She began walking, assuming Sampson would be around the corner, but found another hallway with a light shining from the left about ten paces ahead and an elevator fifteen paces in front of that. She walked forward to find the source of the light was a reinforced window, and on the opposite side stood Detective Sampson.

He looked at her and began speaking, but she couldn't hear a word. She reached into her pocket and pulled out her communication earpiece. Slid it into her ear and motioned for him to do the same.

He obliged and said, "What gives?"

"Appears we're being split up," she said, ever so calmly.

"Yeah, well, I don't like it, not one bit. Is there an elevator on your side?"

She nodded, and he said, "Okay, let's stick to the original plan. Let's meet at the top floor. We'll see what he has in store for us up there."

She nodded and took off for the elevator as he did the same. When she reached it, there was only one button. She pushed it, and the doors parted on well-oiled rollers. She stepped in and took notice of the same floors as the first elevator B – 16. She pressed the button for 16. When the doors were shut, it shot up again. This car stopped much quicker than the first. When the doors reopened, she looked at the placard. *12? What the hell is going on here?*, she thought as she stepped out.

"Sampson," she said into her comms, "can you hear me?"

"I can, but you aren't going to believe this. I pressed the button for the top floor, and it took me down to the fourth."

"Yeah, and I ended up on the twelfth. I'm going to investigate my floor. There's a reason I'm here and you are there. We might as well start solving this puzzle so we can bring this ordeal to an end."

"I'll do the same," he said, orienting himself. "Keep your comms in and relay anything of note."

"Same goes for you. And, Sampson," she said in all sincerity, "watch your back. I have a bad feeling things are just getting started."

As Donatella walked away from the elevator, the doors silently closed behind her. Like other rooms she'd already encountered, the lighting was dim, and crevices were all around. She diligently proceeded through the space, floorboards creaking with each foot placement. She paid close attention to this, as the remainder of the house seemed extremely sturdy. Therefore, there should be no reason for these floorboards to –

Her body went into action before her brain finished processing the thought. She took off in a sprint, gaining speed and momentum with each step. The floor disintegrated behind her seconds after her foot parted from it. With the dim lights casting shadows all over the place, it was impossible to determine openings from dead ends.

Her eyes darted left to right and then right to left, looking for another pathway. She didn't have time to look behind her as she ran, but she could feel heat from behind and the smell of wood burning in her wake. She also began putting some distance between herself and the falling floor.

She continued searching for an avenue of escape, as the end of this corridor was quickly approaching. Her mind registered an opening to the right as she passed by. Her momentum carried her forward, and she quickly turned on her heels and ran back in the direction of the falling floor. She calculated the rate of the floor's disintegration and the distance she needed to cover. *It's going to be close.*

She moved to the center of the floor, her salvation to her left now in clear sight. *Three strides*, she thought, and on the third she leapt. As she flew through the air, the wooden beam on which she took her last step fell into the bubbling inferno below.

The angle of her flight meant she would land in the middle of the adjacent corridor or would clip the edge and fall to her death. With her legs and arms pumping like a long jumper, she feared her calculation was off as her body was heading for the corner. With the control of a gymnast, she willed her body right, and it responded. Her trail foot clipped the corner, which caused her to roll into the parallel wall that brought her to a stop.

She breathed a sigh of relief before scrambling to her feet. When she did, she spotted another elevator tucked away at the end of the hall. She regained her composure, straightened her jacket, and proceeded to the elevator. She pressed the down button, and as she waited on the car to arrive, she contemplated what was going on.

Thus far, the elevator hadn't taken her to the selected floor, and she suspected this would continue to be the case. She filed this away in the back of her mind as the door opened. She stepped in, pressed the button for the second floor, and waited as the doors slowly closed.

DETECTIVE SAMPSON cautiously walked onto the dimly lit fourth floor with his senses on high alert. Separating them had been a strategic move, but the motivation was unclear. The monster had lured them into his lair, and now he wasn't sure how Donatella was fairing. He was battling two thoughts in his head. First, he couldn't live with himself if anything happened to her. Second, if anyone was equipped to take care of themselves, she was the one.

The distinctive faint buzz of lights coming to life could be heard all around him as the floor was flooded with artificial light. He squinted in reaction to his eyes adjusting to the assault on his pupils. Moments later, Sampson was speechless as the floor came into focus.

The ceiling, which would have been the fifth floor, was missing. And yet in the distance he could see what appeared to be a door of some sorts elevated on the far side of the floor. Next, he noticed how wide the floor was. It was void of furniture, rooms, and everything else you'd expect to see. The last thing he noticed was a rope hanging precariously in the center of the space.

A slow and increasing whine reminiscent of a jet engine could be heard coming from the far side of the open room. As it increased in intensity, Sampson could feel a stiff wind pushing against him. Next, he heard a crank turning—no, two cranks turning—on either side of him. He looked to both his left and his right but couldn't identify the source of the sounds.

As the whine built and the wind increased, the rope in the center of the space began to blow in his direction. His senses were screaming danger, but he couldn't yet place a finger on its origin. Unlike the noise coming from in front of him that continued to increase, the cranking sounds from the left and the right stayed consistent. He began walking over to his right to identify the source of the sound. As he walked, he didn't see anything other than the blank wall staring back at him. He stopped and eyed it. In that moment, it hit him what was happening and why his senses were warning him.

As he was walking toward the wall, his depth perception was failing to register anything that was off. But when he stood still, he noticed the wall moving toward him. There was no doubt the other side was doing the same thing. He turned to run for the rope, but his progress was being impeded as he fought the head-on wind.

Fighting the gale was a struggle but not insurmountable, at least not yet. Considering its strength was increasing with each passing moment and with nothing to grab onto, if he didn't reach the rope soon, the danger he was in would become deadly.

From his current position, the rope was forty yards away. The first fifteen were met with mild resistance, akin to walking a steep hill. But as the intensity of the wind increased, each step became exponentially harder. At twenty yards, he turned his head to watch the relentless movement of the wall like the secondhand journeying around a clock.

It took supreme effort for Sampson to lift his right leg, followed by his left. The gravity in the room seemed to have doubled as he struggled to push forward. The walls had now drawn within twenty feet, and he was now five yards from the rope.

The wind played havoc with it, nearly pushing it horizontal. He reached out to secure it, but the wind blew it past his grasp. *Almost*, he thought as he took another step. On his second attempt, he grabbed hold of the bottom of it and used it to pull himself forward. He positioned himself directly beneath the top of the rope affixed to the ceiling two floors up.

Sampson never considered himself an expert rope climber, but he was no slouch. He could tell his legs were spent with the effort to reach the rope, which meant his arms would need to do most of the work. He positioned both hands on the rope, giving it a tug to ensure it would hold his weight. Satisfied it was secured in place, he began to climb.

With his feet off the ground, the wind from the unseen source began battering his body like a rag doll. With his center of gravity in constant motion, it made the climb three times more challenging. He pulled with is right arm and then his left. Forearms burning, biceps bulging. The walls were closing in, and as they drew nearer, it felt they were increasing in speed.

Pulling with his upper body and no support from his legs, his hands were getting rope burns with each action. In the narrow-confined space between the walls, the concentration of the wind turned into a vortex pulling back toward the elevator he exited. Sampson's body banged against one wall and then the other as it took all of his strength to hold on. He could feel his grip loosening, and he knew he had to devise a plan before being smashed between the moving masses.

As his body banged against the walls for a second time, he slipped down the rope, which refocused his mind. A moment of clarity struck, and he had a plan of action. As his body prepared to hit against the wall again, he shifted his body and extended his legs. He bent his knees on impact to lessen the chance he'd bounce completely from the surface.

With the rope taut and feet firmly planted against the moving wall, Sampson angled against the source of the wind and used it to shove him forward. He used what power he had remaining in his lower body to steady himself against the wall as he climbed. The other wall was close to touching his shoulder, and he could see the top. With his arms and legs now working in unison, he fought off the pain and pushed down the realization that the walls were only a few seconds from closing completely.

A foot from the top, he reached both hands over the edge, released the rope, and with all the might he had remaining in his body, he pulled himself over the lip and rolled away from the entrance as it slammed shut.

He collapsed there, splayed out and staring at the ceiling. The ding of the elevator brought him back to the realization that he had a job to do. He pushed himself to his feet, finding it much easier to move around without the wind blowing against him. He stepped on the elevator, pressed the button to the seventh floor, and wondered, *What else does he have in store?*

26

As Donatella climbed into her elevator on the twelfth floor, Sampson was lumbering into his elevator on the fifth. When their respective doors closed, Donatella noticed something she hadn't spotted before, a glint of a camera lens tucked away behind the faux glass on the elevator panel.

For this elevator, she'd selected the second floor, and thus far it was at least going in the right direction. This time when the car stopped and the doors opened, the placard read 3. This misdirection hadn't been a surprise, but this time she approached the floor with a different objective. She quickly scanned her surroundings, looking for the telltale signs of a camera.

Her search immediately borne fruit, as she spotted a camera barely visible in the corner of the room above the elevator. She took a leap of faith that this would not be the only one in the room. She retrieved her phone from her pocket and conferenced BJ into her and Sampson's comms.

"BJ, I need you to track my current location. Sampson

and I are in a building in Uptown Charlotte. The building has closed-circuit surveillance. I need you to tap into it and become our eyes."

"I'm on it," he said. "Give me a few minutes."

Sampson chimed in, sounding winded, "Where are you now?"

"I'm on three after pressing two," she said, venturing out onto the floor.

"I pressed seven and now I'm up on thirteen," he responded. "Stay alert. He doesn't appear to be rolling out the welcome mat."

BJ spoke into the comms, "This may take a little longer than expected. The password requires a key and has multi-factor authentication to gain access. I can bypass it, but I'll need some time."

"Let me know when you've gained access. Carl, be careful." She disconnected and wearily ventured into the space.

This floor was different than the previous ones she encountered. While the others were vast and wide open, this one was full of corridors and right angles. She wasn't sure what to make of it other than that it was another obstacle to overcome.

When she turned the corner, an unseen door slammed closed behind her, and the light brightened two shades. She realized she was surrounded by mirrors everywhere she looked. To her right, her left, the ceiling, and even the door that had closed behind her. Mirrors covered every visible surface. All except the floor.

As she stepped forward, she could see the sliver of an opening diagonal to her position. She proceeded in that direction, tuning her ears for the slightest sound. She forced her eyes to see past her carbon copies staring back at her. She pressed forward.

She came to an opening that had a path to the right and another path to the left. Without hesitation, she chose right. As she walked toward this mirror, she caught a glimpse of the mirror behind her, which gave the unsettling feeling of an infinite tunnel. She ignored the tricks her eyes were beginning to play on her and focused on the path ahead.

When she came to the next bend along the path, she felt a sense of relief. The subtle gap in the mirrors provided the break her eyes needed to regain her spatial awareness. She walked forward another ten steps and reached a dead end. She turned, preparing to head back in the direction she'd come from, when she felt the floor give three inches and heard an audible click. Her brain immediately registered, *Pressure-sensitive switch*.

Her mind raced with the countless possibilities behind the switch and what it meant – all of which were bad. She calculated her options. She could stay here and wait for someone to come find her, which was unlikely. Or she could move her foot to see what would transpire.

The calculations didn't take long, as there was truly only one option. She started choreographing her movements to account for the greatest number of threats. Dropping to the ground and hugging the nearest wall continued to stand out as her best bet, so she settled on this as the best course of action. She counted herself down, and when she silently recited one, she dove to the floor, pressed against the wall, and covered her head.

Surprisingly nothing shot out, and there was no explosion, but she wasn't out of the woods yet. A sound, like a chainsaw, filled the room followed by the opening of the floor behind her.

A series of razor-sharp rotating blades materialized and without provocation started in her direction. She climbed to her feet and rushed to put distance between herself and the murderous blades. The mirrors were causing a bit of disorientation as she retraced her steps. As she ran, the blades increased in speed, nearly slicing her Achilles'. She spotted an opening and darted to her left. As she did, the blades continued their forward motion, stopping mere inches from the mirror. The blades reversed rotation and headed back in the direction they'd come from.

She took a moment to orient herself. She was back at the same intersection at the beginning. As she walked forward, if this was the hall from her recollection, there would be an entrance coming up on her left. A few more steps and she was relieved to find the hall exactly where she thought.

Making the left would take her back where she started, so the correct answer to this mirror maze was to go straight ahead. Donatella understood two important factors. First, she would have to keep a mental map of her surroundings. The room was a maze, and she would have to find the exit. Second, a wrong turn would likely be met with deadly consequences. So, in addition to the mental map, she needed to be prepared to react quickly should she make a wrong turn. She took a deep breath and continued forward.

Donatella followed the maze as it led her deeper into what she assumed was a cavernous space. With each step she took, and every move she made, she listened intently. Although she'd escaped the blades two left turns and three right turns ago, she could still hear them faintly running in the background. The mirrors were still causing her to second guess everything she was seeing, and the walking path seemed way too calm. Then she reached another decision point.

She kept walking straight, where there appeared to be a dogleg left ahead or a right turn. She rationalized any decision made would be a guess, so she continued to move straight and to the slight left turn. She couldn't tell if it was her imagination playing tricks on her or if the space had grown darker and colder. As she continued down the mirror-lined corridor, she had her answer.

Condensation was etching up the mirror, and as she pressed forward, she could see her breath. It wasn't lost on her that the floor had started to become slick with a slight decline. The warning signal in her brain screamed that this was the wrong way, but she was committed to this course of action. And who was to say the cold wasn't a red herring?

She was coming up on another left turn, the chill increasing. She navigated the intersection, making the turn and sliding for her effort. Her natural, smooth, long stride turned to a decreased gait, focus on footing and a heightening of her senses. She was preparing to take her next step when the warning signal went from screaming to flashing a stop sign in her brain.

She paused, taking note of the fact the darkness had become nearly absolute. She retrieved her phone and activated the flashlight. She was surprised to see the step she'd been planning to take was not there. She was at a ledge with nothing but darkness below. She shifted her body weight back to her foot on the ground and placed her other foot cautiously next to it. She slowly turned around to head back in the direction she'd come from. She started walking when she noticed a red glow from the mirror in front of her. Before she could react, a projectile whizzed past her ear, slicing a few strands of hair as it passed.

Its impact against the mirror caused shards of glass to fly across the open space. Instinctively, she knew this wouldn't be the only one and was rewarded with her sound deduction with another projectile flying harmlessly off to her left. She dug her heel into the floor, preparing to make a run for it, but with the slick surface she lost her balance and hit the ground. Her momentum was pulling her back toward the hole as another projectile flew overhead.

She could feel her toes dangling over the edge, followed by her ankles then her shins. Her eyes searched for something to grab a hold of, but nothing presented itself. She reached to her utility belt with her right hand and extracted one of her throwing knives. As she continued to slide into the black pit, she swung her arm over her head and jammed the knife into the floor. Her body stopped sliding. She was able to reach down with her left hand and obtain another knife. She pulled her body forward with her right hand and stabbed the second knife into the floor. As she was doing this, the flying projectiles hadn't stopped, sending two more down the corridor.

She reached back down to her utility belt with her right hand, extracted a third knife, and repeated the process she'd done with the first two. It took a total of five before her entire body was no longer hanging precariously over the edge, but she still had a problem, the flying projectiles and the slippery surface. Staying low to the ground would be her best option, and with the knives she'd left in the floor she could use them as foot holds to keep from sliding back toward the pit.

She allowed her legs to do most of the work to propel her forward. She'd gotten back to the point on the floor where it wasn't as slick but instead was covered in glass shards, and the projectiles kept flying over her. She used her forearms to clear away the broken glass, but some managed to slice through her jacket and draw blood. As she crawled, she became painfully aware that the swiping of the glass had only partially done the job.

She could feel little jagged pieces of glass sticking into her hands as she crawled forward along with pieces still slicing through her jacket. She reached the intersection where she had made the left and finally crawled the last few meters to safety. There she was able to stand up, the projectiles continuing to fly harmlessly past. She had a few deep cuts in her hands, but the rest were superficial. She wiped the glass from her clothing and once again headed back in the direction from which she'd come from.

Donatella consulted her mental map, realizing she would be coming up on the dogleg left she made, which led to yet another trap. She found it useful to play out her memory prior to approaching any junction so she wouldn't be influenced by what she was now seeing and end up getting turned around. After she navigated the upcoming turn, she'd be faced with a diagonal off to the left, which was the right hand turn she passed up or a path straight, which would take her backward.

When she approached the bend, she saw what she expected. She wasted no time taking the diagonal. She followed the path once again, taking rights followed by lefts. She could feel the blood trickling down to her fingertips as she walked, but she ignored it and focused on getting out of this maze.

She laughed a bemused chuckle when she came to yet another intersection. This time it was either straight ahead or left. Having already tried right, she said out loud, "Left it is."

The left led to another right, and she was already steeling herself for another battle against this unrelenting building. She took inventory of herself, and aside from the few cuts she experienced from her last ordeal, she was in pretty good shape. She was ready to take on whatever came next.

She became instantly relieved when what came next was a short hallway that led to another elevator. She pressed the call button and the elevator doors immediately opened. This time she thought, *Why the hell not?* She pressed the button for the thirteenth floor.

SAMPSON EXITED the elevator on thirteen to something that looked almost – normal. For the first time since they entered this godforsaken building, he saw rooms, or at least there were doors that appeared to lead into rooms. He wouldn't be 100% sure until he opened a door and looked. There were defined hallways, and the lighting was at an acceptable level. Yet the normalcy gave him an eerie feeling he couldn't shake.

He walked until he came to the first door, reached out, and tried the knob, *locked.* He couldn't fathom why a door would be locked in a building that up to this point had been trying to kill him. He figured it had to be some sort of mind game and kept moving. When he arrived at the second door, he tried the handle and found that it too was locked. He continued to walk down the hallway, and each door he'd come to had been locked. He turned heading down the next hall, and each of the thirteen rooms on this wing were locked too.

He turned the corner again to find a series of doors on each side of the hallway, like the first two. But this one was different. Directly ahead at the end of the hall was a wall that spanned the entire width. And in the center of the wall was a single, unmarked, wooden door.

Sampson didn't bother with the handles on the side doors, because he knew they would yield the same results. They were for show and nothing more. He was being led to the entrance at the end. He walked past each door, laser focused on the one directly ahead of him. When he reached it, he stuck out his hand, turned the knob, and walked in.

The motion sensor lights kicked on to reveal a room that was much smaller than expected. But the lights didn't illuminate the entire room, only the center. And sitting in the center were four easels each with a dedicated spotlight shining onto them. Sampson noted a white sheet covered each one, and he knew what this psychopath wanted. Sampson had the power to deprive him of his wish by simply leaving each sheet in place. And yet he was drawn to find out what was beneath each one. He weighed the options, convincing himself to move on and proceed to the next room. But he rationalized that there wasn't a next room. This floor was meant for him, its sole purpose to guide him to this room.

Reluctantly, he went to the one on the left. The silence in the room was broken by the loud beating of his heart. He stilled himself and removed the covering. Staring back at him was a four by three foot canvas that was split horizontally across the middle. On the top half was the photo of Mandy Cox that had been used for her "Missing" poster. The engaging smile, bright eyes, and a life cut short. Beneath that picture was a crime scene photo of her skinned body that had been left out for all to see.

Sampson could feel the rage simmering as he said another prayer for her soul and moved to the next easel. Although his heart was beating faster than when he'd uncovered the first one, he didn't waste any time uncovering the second. Like the first, this too was split in half horizontally. The top, the high school senior picture Brianna Armstrong's mom had given to the local news to run a reward for her safe return, a reward no one collected. At the bottom was the picture of her body in the abandoned warehouse skinned and seated in the chair.

Sampson closed his eyes, put his head in his hands, and took a deep breath. She hadn't deserved this. Had he solved the monster's mystery, she would still be alive. He asked her departed soul for forgiveness, knowing that he would never forgive himself. The rage that had been simmering had turned into a slow boil.

He stepped over to the third one, painfully aware what would be awaiting him under the white sheet. Once again, he pondered simply leaving the cover in place, removing the control Troy had and going to finish this once and for all. But he couldn't. He needed to feel this pain because the victims could no longer feel. He knew his pain, in this moment, could be redirected to do what needed to be done.

He pulled the sheet. Only one picture. One shining face looking back at him. Detective Porter's academy graduation picture with her in her dress blues. It was the picture that stood next to her casket. The picture he stared at after the twenty-one-gun salute. He clinched his fist as the slow boiling rage threatened to boil over. Porter was one of the good ones. She didn't deserve what happened to her.

He looked back at each picture. Mandy, Brianna, Elise. None of them deserved any of this. He heard the request from Bethany Evans, but he wasn't in the mood to forgive. He wasn't in the mindset to forget. Right now, all he could feel was the need for retribution.

He glared at the remaining white sheet ominously sitting atop the final easel. His legs for the second time today felt like cement as he maneuvered in front of it. He had no idea what he would see. Nonetheless, he took a deep breath and tugged. It hit the ground at about the same time his heart followed suit.

On the last canvas was a still photo of Donatella in the rain at Carowinds. The shot captured her walking toward Demon's Breath with individual droplets of rain suspended in animation around her. His breath caught in his chest making it hard to breathe. Sampson's head was spinning as the realization hit. He intended for Donatella to be the next victim.

The remaining lights came to life, revealing a second door in the room. Sampson reacted on instinct. He ran to the door, his mind focused on saving Donatella. Three feet from the door, he felt a panel click under his foot. The baseboards on each wall rose, and for what seemed like a lifetime, nothing happened, until he removed his foot from the floor panel. Instantly water began gushing from the baseboard openings and into the room.

Sampson reached out and grabbed the handle to the door, *locked*. He raced back to the door that gave him entry into this room, *locked.* He frantically searched only to find there were no other exits from this room. He felt the water splashing against his feet as he tried pulling at the first door and then the second. Neither would budge.

Donatella activated the comms, "I'm now on the thirteenth floor."

Sampson couldn't believe his luck. He said, "Good. I'm still here. You can ignore the doors, because they're locked. I'm trapped in the room at the dead end, and it's currently filling with water."

Donatella responded, "Sampson, I don't see any doors."

27

When the elevator stopped and the doors opened, the last thing Donatella expected to see on the placard was 13. Up to this point, the elevator took them to the floor of its choosing. With the elevator stopping on thirteen, the last floor Sampson reported in from, she began to feel uneasy. Unlike the previous floors, this one was perfectly lit with open rooms all around.

The first room she came to was reminiscent of a home's family room. Top-tier red leather sofa and loveseat. Wooden coffee table with end tables anchoring the couches. Plush carpeting covered the floor from wall-to-wall and the fireplace blazed in the background. Donatella stepped in far enough to clear the room before she proceeded forward.

The next room varied wildly from the first. Where the previous room was homely and inviting, this room was empty and cold. The only decoration, if you could call it that, was an axe situated on the wall across from the entrance. Again, she did her due diligence. She entered the room and verified it was indeed empty.

She carried on for a few minutes walking through the hallways and clearing the variety of rooms that presented themselves. She realized in her shock of landing on the floor she selected and the normal feel to the area that she hadn't contacted Sampson. It had been a while since he checked in.

"I'm now on the thirteenth floor," she said after activating her comms. A few moments passed before Sampson responded.

"Good. I'm still here. You can ignore the doors, because they're locked. I'm trapped in the room at the dead end, and it's currently filling with water."

Donatella's thoughts started racing as every room she passed had been completely open. She picked up her pace and said, "Sampson, I don't see any doors."

"What do you mean you don't see any doors? When you exit the elevator, you are in a corridor filled with rooms on each side. Each one had the door closed and the latch locked. If I recall correctly, there were thirteen rooms on each wing."

Donatella began to sprint. She was obsessive compulsive about numbers and counting. She'd recognized the oddity of the thirteen rooms as well. She thought back to each of the floor she had encountered. Each had a second elevator to exit through after completing the puzzle. It stood to reason Sampson entered on one elevator while she had entered from the other. If they both entered on separate elevators, what nefarious puzzle needed to be solved for them to exit this floor?

"I'm coming to you," she said, legs churning and arms

pumping. She took a right followed by a left when she'd come to a dead end with a door situated in the center. She ran to it and pounded, "Sampson, are you in there?"

"Yeah," he said, "I'm happy to hear your voice. Now unlock the door and let me out of here."

The relief she felt in finding Sampson was quickly replaced with dread. "There isn't a lock or a handle," she said, letting her head fall to the door. She knew in this moment that this was the puzzle.

"Okay," Sampson said, "the water's up to my shoulders and rising quickly. I'd say the ceiling is fourteen, maybe fifteen feet tall. We need to think quickly."

BJ, who'd been listening in and frantically working in the background to infiltrate the private network supplying the camera feed said, "I'm in and have you both. What can I do to help?"

"Search the cameras on the rest of this floor. See if there is anything –" She stopped in mid-sentence.

"I lost you," BJ said. "Please retransmit." But she was already in motion before the words finished exiting his mouth.

Special Agent Donatella sprinted at top speed, retracing her path through the labyrinth of hallways. In a room on the left, she idly recalled an axe decorating the wall that could be of assistance.

"Hold on, Carl," she implored, finding the room and crossing its threshold. She rushed across the vast emptiness and tugged at the axe, devastated to find it tightly fixed to the wall. For leverage, she situated her right foot against the wall and pulled with all her might. The cuts in her hands began to bleed again, with droplets falling to the floor. Her biceps bulged and back muscles activated with the strenuous effort, yet the axe remained in place.

Frustration and anxiety began to rise, but she refused to give it life. She placed her left foot on the wall, joining her right, and positioned them shoulder-width apart. Again, she pulled at the axe, and this time she could feel the back end of the axe beginning to shift followed by the front. Her breaths were growing progressively labored with this effort on top of what she expended on the trials she'd gone through to get to this point.

The only thought running through her mind was that she needed to save him. After everything they had gone through, she wouldn't lose him, not now. She closed her eyes, dug her heels into the wall, took a deep breath, tightened all the muscles from her legs to her arms, and with a primordial yell, she pulled at the axe.

With a loud resounding crack, it detached from the stud, and the action sent Donatella flying across the room, falling to the floor in a heap.

She stood, heaved the axe over her shoulder, and immediately took off in a sprint. "How much time do I have?" she asked BJ after activating her comms.

"You better hurry," he said matter-of-factly.

Outside the chamber of death, the monitor relayed the precarious situation playing out in real-time on the other side of the door.

Sampson's head was now touching the ceiling as he waded in water that had risen to his shoulders.

"If you're going to do something, it better be now," BJ said with increased urgency.

Donatella, who was nearly out on her feet, balanced the

axe in both hands and swung. She made solid contact with the door and was rewarded with two realizations.

First, the wood gave way upon impact, and she could easily make short work of it.

Second, the wood was an outer shell covering a metal door.

Fighting denial, she swung again only to hear the *ting* of metal against metal. Refusing to give up, she swung again and again, keenly aware of the insanity of it all. She dropped the axe and subsequently fell to her knees.

She helplessly eyed the monitor, finding the water was just below Sampson's mouth. She watched as Carl took a deep breath and disappeared beneath the surface.

Donatella pounded her fist on the floor, once, twice, three times, furious that she failed. She wouldn't allow Sampson's death to be in vain. All bets were off. Troy would be brought to justice in what way she saw fit. She was preparing to stand when the floor beneath her gave way, and she found herself falling through the darkness.

28

Donatella didn't know how far she'd fallen before she came to rest on a stuntman's airbag. She opened her eyes to find she was in complete darkness. Prior to making any movements, she blinked her eyes slowly three times If memory served her correctly, this would activate the night vision equipped in BJ's contact lenses.

Opening her eyes after the third blink brought the room into focus, albeit with green hues, eradicating the darkness around her. She climbed down from the airbag and looked from left to right in an effort orient herself. Behind her was a wall, which meant the only path was forward.

With the aid of her night vision, she noted the emptiness of the floor, just walls and corners. Her gut told her this was the end game and that there wouldn't be any additional traps waiting. From reviewing the case and reading the profile from Special Agent Browning, Troy liked to be hands-on with his victims. Therefore, with Sampson now out of the way, he'd have his one-on-one opportunity with Donatella, something he would certainly regret.

She threw caution to the wind and strode with purpose. She was anxious to come face-to-face with Troy and to bring this overdue ordeal to an end. To think of the lives he'd taken when he appeared to be an ordinary man. A stable job. A wife who loved him. A daughter who in her young age adored him. Yet he was filled with these demons that pushed him to abduct, murder, and mutilate young women. Demons that caused him to throw it all way.

She continued walking with more force behind each step as she thought about the lives he cut short, the families that were now broken and the betrayal that would never be forgiven. She clenched her fist as the blood continued to flow from her open cuts.

She turned the corner and entered a room in which a form stood still in the middle. She paused when she realized she had finally reached the mastermind behind this debacle, Troy Evans. He watched her, as she stared back at him.

The room was still dark, so she wasn't sure if he could see her. It would be so easy for her to pull her SIG Sauer P226 from her holster and put him down like the monster he was. She could avenge the women who'd lost their lives. She could avenge the loss of Carl. But as much as that would help her feel better, she'd never taken a life unless she was defending hers or someone else's.

The way he stood off at the distance gave the impression he hadn't seen her but that he was certainly awaiting her arrival. She saw no need in belaboring the point. She started off in his direction once again when her eyes were assaulted with bright lights. She closed them tight, as they burned from the overhead lights activating in the room. She waited the five seconds, plus two additional, to deactivate the night vision. When she reopened them, Troy was no longer standing in front of her.

She sensed movement behind her and to the left, but before she could react, she felt an electrical current flowing through her body, seizing her muscles and causing her body to fall to the floor. The pain didn't stop until she was completely sprawled out. She could feel the control she normally exhibited over her body draining with each passing second until finally all control was gone.

Troy pulled her pliant arms behind her back and placed flex cuffs to her wrists. He said, "So nice of you to join me today, Agent Donatella. I must admit, I didn't see this going so splendidly well. To think, I was able to ensnare perhaps the most decorated FBI agent in one of my traps. I have officially ascended."

She was still feeling the effects of the voltage running through her body. She was equipped with the ability to free herself from the cuffs, but only if she could regain full use of her limbs. She needed to keep him talking.

"So you were willing to throw away your marriage for what? This?"

"Marriage. I loved Beth, but she was beginning to turn into one of them."

Them, she wondered.

He continued, "She was no longer the woman I married. But I spared her because I love her."

"And what about your daughter?"

"Everything I've done, I did for her. She couldn't grow up in a world where people can get away with things just by batting an eye or flirting, especially the blondes. They were the worst of the bunch, just like my mother. But I showed her. And the world is much better off without her."

Donatella's head was spinning as his words were coming out in a jumbled rush.

"Okay, so how did Detective Porter fit into all of this?" She could feel the tingle in her toes.

"Well, that was his plan, sort of like this one. The girls were no challenge, but they had to go. But you and Porter. You both were worthy of the hunt."

His plan, she thought, *so there is someone else pulling the strings now. That would explain the reason for the change in MO.*

"Who's plan?" she asked, now able to flex her foot.

Troy's head snapped around to face her, and in a deep voice she hadn't recognized, he said, "Mine."

His facial features hardened, matching the new voice, and his eyes darkened as he glared at her. She stared back, fully comprehending what was happening. The muscles on his face relaxed, and his eyes cleared.

"I'm sorry. What was that?" he asked, moving her to a seated position and ensuring her bonds were tight. "Anyway, we need to wait for our guest to arrive. We wouldn't want him to miss the show."

Her head was completely spinning now. Was he referring to a physical embodiment of someone else or just the second personality living within Troy?

"Troy, who are we waiting on?" she asked, trying to make sense of his latest comment.

He was once again facing her when the hard edges returned, and a sadistic smile appeared on his face. He pulled her to her feet, and with him supporting most of her weight, she was able to stand. An elevator dinged off to her left, and Troy turned them so they'd be facing the person exiting.

When the doors opened the soaking figure of Detective Carl Sampson emerged.

29

Donatella could hardly believe her eyes as Sampson staggered off the elevator. She was mixed with a series of emotions, the top of which was confusion. She had watched him drown before she ended up taking a free fall to this floor. How had he survived? Or, worse, was he in on this from the beginning?

Could this have been the reason the cases were never solved? Could this be why Troy was able to get away with this? She shook her head, as none of it made sense. He was the one who came to her seeking help to find the killer and to bring him to justice. Troy's words echoed through her mind.

"Well, that was his plan, sort of like this one. The girls were no challenge, but they had to go. But you and Porter, you both were worthy of the hunt."

Porter and I had been worthy of the hunt, she thought as Sampson drew nearer. She refused to believe he was in on this. It couldn't be true. But here he was, alive and well after he was to have drowned.

"Drop the syringe," Sampson said, holding his Glock 43x with the attached laser scope.

The deep voice emerged from Troy once again, "Welcome, Detective. You are late as usual."

"I said drop it," Sampson said again, hate dripping from his tone.

Donatella still lacked full sensation from her body, which was why she hadn't noticed the needle pressed against her neck.

"I'm not going to do that," Troy's second personality said. "You have no cards to play, and I hold the winning hand. You see the opening over to your right." He tipped his head in that direction.

Sampson momentarily moved his eyes off Troy and looked.

"It's the antidote to the nasty concoction I have formulated in this vial. The ledge that's holding it up is tied to my heartbeat. If my heart stops, it drops. The antidote will hit the ground, and your chance of saving her will die with me. You've failed so many times. Don't you want to win at least this once?"

Sampson held the Glock steady. "Or I could simply shoot you now, before you depress the plunger, and I wouldn't need to worry about any of this."

He smiled. "I bet you were fooled by every magic trick you've ever seen. Don't you know the first rule in magic, misdirection?"

The arm that had been holding Donatella steady lifted, and Troy's hand held an empty syringe.

"She's already been given the injection. So, what are you going to do now?"

He let her body fall to the ground and backed away. For

the first time in the exchange, Donatella saw the indecisiveness in Sampson's face.

An elevator opened up behind them, and she could sense Troy walking away.

"Kill him," Donatella said, without hesitation.

Sampson looked down at her, and Troy continued backing toward the elevator.

"Do it now before he escapes," she said once again. "Don't worry about me. Take the shot."

Sampson's eyes left hers and found Troy's. He fired three shots, one between the eyes, two center mass. Troy crumpled to the ground, and seconds later the glass tube tucked away on the side shattered against the ground.

Sampson holstered his gun and ran to Donatella. He leaned over, and she said, "Help me up. We need to get out of here. Our best bet is to head for the elevator Troy was planning to take. It's probably the best path out of here."

BJ spoke on the comms, "I've pinpointed your position and have sent for the EMTs. I also noticed Jasmyn is in the area. I'm sending her to your location as well."

Donatella didn't want to know how BJ knew Jasmyn's whereabouts, but they were seriously going to have to discuss boundaries.

Sampson helped Donatella to her feet and used his knife to cut her bindings. They took three steps, and she collapsed. Her eyes were closed, and her breathing was becoming erratic. He hefted her into a fireman's carry and raced to the elevator.

"BJ, she's passed out. How far out are they?"

"About five minutes, but you don't have that long. I show Troy had a failsafe. There's a countdown timer in the control room, and it's down to a minute and forty-six seconds."

Sampson stepped into the elevator, and there was only one button. He pressed it, willing the doors to close and the car to start moving.

They rose only one floor before the doors opened. Sampson immediately recognized the floor as the first one. He hurried toward the exit, willing his legs to keep him steady. At the door, he reached for the handle, turned it, and nothing.

He thought back to when they first entered the building, the sound of locks moving into place.

"BJ, the exit door is locked. I believe it's tied into the system. You need to find a way to unlock it."

By the calculation he had running in his head, they were down to less than a minute before the timer would expire.

"Looking," BJ said with a ting of panic.

"It's going to be okay. You're going to make it. I won't lose you." Sampson looked down at the near lifeless body of Donatella. "Dammit, BJ, hurry up." He could feel the clock ticking down. He closed his eyes and silently prayed for a miracle.

The locks to the door disengaged. "Go," BJ said over the comms.

Sampson turned the handled and pulled. The door swung open, and he was greeted with rain falling from the sky and humidity in the air. This hadn't stopped the concert from progressing, as the artist was singing another top song, "SOS."

Sampson ran across the street, screaming at the

bystanders, "Move back! Move away from the building. It's going to blow!"

The crowd started to disperse as Sampson continued across the street as fast as his weary legs would carry him. A loud explosion started at the top of the building followed by one in the middle and then near the foundation. The blast knocked Sampson and others nearby to the ground.

His ears were ringing, and everything began moving in slow motion. A hand grabbed him by his shoulder. His reaction time was off, and he would be unable to ward off any danger. He turned to see Jasmyn Thompson's lips moving, but he couldn't hear a word. He pointed in the direction of Donatella as he tried to shake the cobwebs from his head.

He could feel the blood pressing against his eardrums as he mopped the mixture of rain, sweat, and concrete dust from his brows. He watched helplessly as Nurse Jasmyn did her best to revive her good friend and his new...

Where the hell is that ambulance? he thought, anxiously awaiting its arrival. He could hear the sirens whirring in the distance, but they didn't appear to be getting any closer.

"Come on, Donatella," he said, pounding the ground soaked in rain and mud. "You can't let this son of a bitch win!"

With the flurry of activity they endured, he hadn't taken inventory of himself or his injuries and soon realized with the impact that he'd dislocated his shoulder. The adrenaline coursing through his body had negated the pain, but the dull ache was preparing to emerge as excruciating pain.

The reflection of the lights emanating from the ambulance cleared his thoughts. "They're here," he exclaimed, pushing himself to his feet and blocking away the pain. He waved them down as they approached and slowed to a stop.

Out of habit, he reached for his shield before recalling he didn't have it. "Detective Sampson," he said behind clenched teeth. "Hurry, she's right here." He pointed the emergency crew in the direction of Jasmyn, who was hunched over the prone, motionless form of Donatella.

With practiced motion, the pair opened the rear doors and retrieved the gurney.

Jasmyn stood and spoke, "Black female, age twenty-nine, excellent physical health. Injected with unknown substance, currently unresponsive but still breathing."

The techs maneuvered her into position and quickly strapped her into place. They lifted it back to full height and began rolling it to the ambulance.

"Thanks, we've got it from here," one of the techs said as they slid the gurney into the back.

"I'm coming with you," Jasmyn said as they prepared to climb in. "I'm a nurse at Atrium and the victim's friend. I can lend a hand."

The techs shot each other a glance and wordlessly agreed to the request.

"So am I," Sampson said as Jasmyn climbed in.

"Wait a minute," the tech said, "we don't have the room and aren't allowed to have civilians riding with us."

"Make the room," he said in a cold, menacing tone.

The tech parted her lips to say something but thought better of it and simply slid to the side to let him enter.

By the time he was in and the door was closed, Donatella's shirt had been cut open and EKG leads had been placed across her chest. Her pulse was thready, and her blood pressure was spiking.

In the bright lights, he could see how much color had drained from her face. *Come on, fight*, he thought as he watched them work.

The activity picked up suddenly, and distantly he heard Jasmyn shout, "We're losing her."

His eyes grew wide, and a ping of pain registered in his chest. *Not again, not another one.* His mind flashed back to when Porter was in an ambulance fighting for her life and how helpless he'd been to save her.

He watched as Jasmyn fought to insert an IV into her vein. His focus shifted to the ever-slowing heart rate monitor and the rhythm that decreased with each subsequent beat of her heart.

His eyes turned back to Jasmyn and the techs as their urgency reached a fevered pitch. Guilt began to creep into his mind for placing her in the path of this psychopath. If only...

The slow, rhythmic report from the heart monitor beeped once more before giving way to the monotoned flatline. Sampson could feel his heart stop. He couldn't believe it happened again. He lost another partner, and this time it was someone he really cared about. He dropped his head in disbelief.

When Jasmyn and the EMTs stopped working, he wanted to demand them to keep trying, but he knew it was no use. She was gone, and there was nothing he could do about it.

The smartwatch on Donatella's wrist kicked into action. The needle pricked her skin and sent the full allotment of adrenaline and other fluids into her system. Immediately, her vitals began to spike, sending the heart rate monitor into overdrive.

Sampson was the first to react, lifting his head in disbelief. The EMTs and Jasmyn looked at each other uncomprehendingly. Jasmyn finally managed to insert the IV while the tech worked to retrieve antibiotics.

Donatella opened her eyes and said to Sampson, "We made it out."

Sampson looked at her and said, "Yes, we did. We certainly did."

EPILOGUE

"Sampson and Donatella were the only ones to leave the building," Lawson said as she sat in Susan Yates's office. "It's highly unlikely that Troy Evans survived, as there were no other egresses from the building, at least none that we could find."

"So, we still don't know how Veronica King and he were connected," Susan asked, tapping her fingertips on the table.

"No, we don't, but we did uncover that Sampson and Donatella were after him because of the serial killings happening in the city. He's suspected to be the person behind each of them."

Susan raised an eyebrow. "Well, that was unexpected. Nothing to be done about that now."

"I ask you again, what do you want us to do about King?"

Susan thought about it for a moment and returned the same verdict. "Nothing. Whatever game she's playing, it'll be made clear soon enough. Until then, I don't want to let her know that we suspect her of anything. If she's up to something, I want to know if there's anyone else involved or if she's a solo act."

Lawson hid her displeasure with the decision but would play along. King was becoming too much of a lose cannon, one that could do more damage if left untamed. But Lawson believed in the command-and-control structure and would do as she was told.

"Very well. In the meantime, is there anything else you need from me?"

"Make sure to keep your team sharp and prepared. I suspect we'll have something coming our way really soon."

Lawson had become used to these vague statements. Susan would keep the details close to the vest until it was time to engage. So she'd keep the team ready while she ran the daily activities of the FBI's Charlotte field office.

AFTER RUNNING tests and verifying that her vitals were in range, the doctors reluctantly cleared Donatella. She advised them that she would not stay in the hospital and would be leaving regardless of if they cleared her. Although her doctor preferred for her to stay overnight for observations, she simply told them if she was feeling bad that she'd drive herself back.

Before going home, Sampson drove her by the Thompsons' residence, where Jasmyn, Marcellous, and the Grandsons were consoling Bethany. When Donatella and Sampson arrived, she'd cried through all her tears.

Donatella said, "I'm sorry we couldn't save him. He was determined to end it all, and there was nothing more we could do. He brought down the building in the center of Uptown with explosives."

Bethany shook her head in disbelief.

"But I think I know what happened. Had Troy every been diagnosed with any mental disorder?"

She shook her head. "No. Never."

"Well, it appears he was suffering from a psychotic break. When I was with him, just before the end, a second personality arrived with a different demeanor and a deeper voice."

Bethany looked at her. "A deeper voice? One day I was standing outside of his office, and I could have sworn I heard a second voice. A deeper voice. But when I walked in, it was just him. He assured me he wasn't talking to anyone, and I let it go. How could I have been so stupid to miss the signs?"

"You weren't, and you aren't. It seems Troy was fighting his demons and was unaware when the second personality had come out." She neglected to mention the part about his mother and the fact he'd thought she changed and was becoming like the women he had killed. She did what she could to preserve a good memory for his wife that she could tell her daughter, even though he had a monster within him. In the end, she felt Bethany had suffered enough.

After finishing up at the Thompsons' residence, she had Sampson drive her home.

"Thank you again for your help," he said, standing with her at the door. "I never would have been able to crack this case without you."

"We had some help," she said.

"We did, but your guidance led us in the right direction. Thank you."

She nodded and said, "And thank you for saving my life. You got us out of that damn building. I never thought I'd be so happy to wake up inside an ambulance." She leaned over and kissed him on the cheek.

"The pleasure's all mine," he said prior to walking back to his car and driving off.

Now as she sat in her solitude, with the only sound coming from the fireplace crackling, she pulled the unopened package from Terri Buckley that she had been putting off opening. But now the minute for excuses had come to an end. It was time to see what game her deceased former FBI partner was playing. She tore open the package, reached in, and removed the contents. Before she looked at them, she thought back to the two clues Terri provided to kick off the hunt for this package.

"Clue number one. Those you consider enemies may hold the key to your salvation, while those you consider friends may be enemies in disguise. If you don't look at this with unclouded eyes, you will never find the answer.

"Clue number two. Inside the envelop, I left you a key to a box. It holds information that you may find useful, but alas it's up to you to find what the key unlocks. It's a dossier I put together specifically for you."

Donatella turned over the dossier and began to read.

"Well, it appears your smarter than the average bear, but who are we kidding? We both know how smart you are, which is why it amazes me you haven't been able to find out who is running The Syndicate. They are the organization responsible for robbing you of your childhood. Since you haven't been able to figure it out for yourself, I'm here to point you in the right direction. But first, it's important for you to understand how you rise through the ranks within the organization.

"You can only rise to the head position if you are willing to make a tremendous sacrifice. That sacrifice is killing what you love most. It's how they ensure you are serious about the organization before passing the reigns over to you. Every leader of the organization has had to do this, without exception.

"The current leader has been in place well over a decade and has amassed a tremendous amount of power, so much so that no one has come close to ascending to that position. I'm sure you're asking yourself what this has to do with you.

"Donatella, it's time you took the blinders off and see what's been in front of you this entire time. You already know The Syndicate is responsible for the death of your parents. But something that high profile is typically requested by a client. Our clientele likes to stay under the radar whenever possible.

"If the killing of your parents didn't come from a client, then who orchestrated their deaths? I'm sure if you'd remove the blinders and put that big brain of yours to work, you'd come up with a name. In fact, I'm willing to bet you have one in mind. So, tell me, Donatella, who's name did you come up with?"

Donatella closed her eyes and allowed the words she just read to repeat in her mind. Terri may have been a sociopath, but she'd never been a liar. The final question echoed one last time.

"So, tell me, Donatella, who's name did you come up with?"

A tear ran from her closed eyes, and she said out loud, "Aunt Susan."

IF YOU ENJOYED "ERADICATING DARKNESS," please consider leaving a **review** so that other readers just like you can locate this novel.

NOTES FROM THE AUTHOR

Thank you for your purchase and taking the time to read Eradicating Darkness, the fifth book in the Donatella Series. Your continued support means the world to me, and you are the reason I continue penning novel after novel.

This installment has been in the making since the events of, Hour of Reckoning. Detective Sampson, Troy Evans, and Bethany Evans were all introduced with the knowledge that they would come back in this novel. I knew back then that I wanted a crossover event between the Donatella Series and the Detective Sampson Series that would focus on apprehending the serial killer from the latter.

Writing both novels at the same time was my largest undertaking as an author and challenged me in ways that the other novels hadn't. In fact, I had to create a color-coded excel document to keep both stories in alignment. But, creating a story in which the serial killer would be identified and dealt with was only the tip of the iceberg.

Continuing the story of Veronica King and her desire to

take over The Syndicate had to play a vital role. She continues to make waves that ruffling some feathers and the question is, has she bitten off more than she can chew. Or will she devise a plan that will oust Susan Yates and find a way to take the helm as her own.

If you haven't done so yet, be sure you are subscribed to my **newsletter** to stay informed of what's coming and obtain access to content only available for those subscribed. Thank you once again for your continued support.

Sincerely
 Demetrius Jackson

This book is a work of fiction. Names, characters, places or incidents are products of the author's imagination and are used fictitiously. Any resemblance to actual events or persons, living or dead, is entirely coincidental.

Eradicating Darkness

Copyright © 2024 by Shadow World Productions, LTD. All rights reserved. No part of this book may be reproduced in any form, except for the inclusion of brief quotations in a review, without permission in writing from the author or publisher.

The scanning, uploading, and distribution of this book without written permission is a theft of the authors' intellectual property. If you would like to use materials from this book (other than for review purposes), prior written permission must be obtained by contacting the publisher at permissions@shadowworldproductions.com. Thank you for your support of the authors' rights.

First edition: May 2024

ISBN 978-1-956355-03-1 (paperback)

❀ Created with Vellum

Made in the USA
Columbia, SC
08 December 2024